P9-EKW-888

BYE-BYE,
EVIL EYE

CALGARY PUBLIC LIBRARY

NOV - - 2014

Also by Deborah Kerbel

FICTION
Mackenzie, Lost and Found (2008)
Girl on the Other Side (2009)
Lure (2010)
Under the Moon (2012)

NON-FICTION
Money Savvy Kids (with Gordon Pape) (2013)

Bye-Bye, Evil Eye

Deborah Kerbel

Copyright © 2014 Deborah Kerbel
This edition copyright © 2014 Dancing Cat Books,
an imprint of Cormorant Books Inc.

No part of this publication may be reproduced, stored in a retrieval system
or transmitted, in any form or by any means, without the prior written consent
of the publisher or a licence from The Canadian Copyright Licensing Agency
(Access Copyright). For an Access Copyright licence,
visit www.accesscopyright.ca or call toll free 1.800.893.5777.

 Canada Council Conseil des Arts    ONTARIO ARTS COUNCIL
for the Arts   du Canada   CONSEIL DES ARTS DE L'ONTARIO
                                        50 YEARS OF ONTARIO GOVERNMENT SUPPORT OF THE ARTS
                                        50 ANS DE SOUTIEN DU GOUVERNEMENT DE L'ONTARIO AUX ARTS

 Canadian Patrimoine   Canadä
Heritage   canadien

The publisher gratefully acknowledges the support of the
Canada Council for the Arts and the Ontario Arts Council for its publishing
program. We acknowledge the financial support of the Government of Canada
through the Canada Book Fund (CBF) for our publishing activities, and the
Government of Ontario through the Ontario Media Development Corporation,
an agency of the Ontario Ministry of Culture,
and the Ontario Book Publishing Tax Credit Program.

LIBRARY AND ARCHIVES CANADA CATALOGUING IN PUBLICATION

Kerbel, Deborah, author
Bye-bye, evil eye / Deborah Kerbel.

Issued in print and electronic formats.
ISBN 978-1-77086-394-1 (pbk.). — ISBN 978-1-77086-395-8 (epub).—
ISBN 978-1-77086-396-5 (mobi)

I. Title.

PS8621.E75B94 2014   JC813'.6   C2013-907908-4
                                      C2013-907909-2

Cover photo and design: Angel Guerra / Archetype
Interior text design: Tannice Goddard, Soul Oasis Networking
Printer: Trigraphik LBF

Printed and bound in Canada.

DANCING CAT BOOKS
An imprint of Cormorant Books Inc.
10 ST. MARY STREET, SUITE 615, TORONTO, ONTARIO, M4Y 1P9
www.dancingcatbooks.com
www.cormorantbooks.com

MIX
Paper from
responsible sources
FSC® C107923

For Barry,
Opener of doors, fixer of words, guru of all things bookish.
With thanks.

GREECE

Chapter 1

· · · · · ·

"I think I see it!"

I crane my neck as I peer out the small oval window, trying to spot a glimpse of the city below. A moment later, it rolls into view just ahead of the shadow of our plane. Clusters of white-washed homes and ribbons of roads surrounded by scrubby hills and mountains. And somewhere down there in that jumble is that old Greek building we learned about in history class. The Parthenon? Or is it the Acropolis? Or are they the same thing? Whatever. You know what I'm talking about.

With my eyes fixed on the scenery, I tap the glass with my pen. "There it is — look. It's Athens!" I lean back into my seat so Kat can see too.

"Cool," she says, peering across my lap. But I can tell from her tone that she's pretending to be impressed for my benefit. And I guess I understand why. After all, she's already been to

Greece five times in her life. But for me, this is a huge thrill. In all my almost fourteen years, I've never left Canada before, let alone flown over an ocean. Or even seen an ocean, for that matter.

I flip to a fresh page in my journal. *Dear Mom, you'll be happy to know that our plane just flew over something very ancient and ruined. It was probably once really important ...*

"The captain is about to begin his descent into Athens," announces a female voice over the droning hum of the engines. "Local time is 2:25 pm. This concludes our flight. Enjoy your stay in Greece and thank you for flying with Canada-Air."

In the middle of her French version, I begin to hear a sound like a bowl of Rice Krispies popping in my ears. A few seconds later, the sound morphs into pain. Raising my hand, I catch the attention of a passing flight attendant.

"Excuse me? Can I get a piece of candy, please?" I ask, smiling my sweetest smile while I point to my ears.

He returns my smile. "Of course. Right away."

Kat holds up her finger. "Could I get one als—"

But he's gone before she can finish her sentence. I shrug. "Sorry, Kat, didn't know you wanted one. I'll ask for another when he comes back."

She nods and slumps back into her seat. Her mother, who's sitting next to the aisle, peers at me over the top of her Greek newspaper. "We'll be landing soon, girls. Please start packing up."

Pack up? But there's still at least twenty more minutes

before landing. Kat dutifully leans over and stuffs her magazine into the front pouch of her carry-on bag. I smile when I spot a few of her contraband romance novels hidden in there.

"*Now* please, Daniella," Mrs. P says. I swallow the protest that's rising in my throat and flip my journal closed with a slap. "Yes, Mrs. Papadakis," I sigh, tucking it into my backpack and capping my pen. Our trip's barely begun and my mother's warning is still fresh in my head.

Kat's mom will be your chaperone on this trip. I'd like you to show her respect and listen to her the entire time.

It was one of only two conditions Mom laid down in return for letting me fly across an ocean to spend three weeks on a sun-soaked Mediterranean island. The other condition was that I learn stuff about Greek culture and history and keep a journal about it all. So, of course, I agreed. Wouldn't you? Even though I knew spending time with Mrs. P wasn't going to be easy. She's one of those strict, old-school moms. I knew it the second I met her last Christmas. She was baking bread when Kat and I walked into the kitchen of their Toronto home after our first tutoring session. The bread was my first tipoff. *Do people still bake their own bread?*

"Mummy, this is my new friend Dani Price," Kat said. Mrs. Papadakis looked up from her dough. The look on her face was like she'd been sucking on a lemon. "Dani? But that's a boy's name," she said in Greek-accented English. "Who would call a girl by a name like that?"

Whoa. Nice to meet you too. "Well, it's really Daniella," I said. "But my parents and everyone just call me Dani — like, since the day I was born."

Her lips stayed pursed as she dusted the flour off her hands. "It's very nice to meet you, *Daniella.*"

Beside me, Kat turned pale. "Mummy, stop," she said under her breath. I waved my hand like it was no big deal. I knew how badly she'd wanted to make a good impression on me. Fact is, she's not that popular, and I am. Yeah, I know that probably sounds conceited, but it's the way it is.

As we left the kitchen, I patted her sympathetically on the shoulder. "Don't worry about it. My grandma Rose is the same. Lots of old people don't like to shorten names."

She turned to me and flashed a grateful smile. Because I didn't want to hurt her feelings, I stopped myself from saying the words that were sitting on the tip of my tongue: that my mother was the complete opposite of hers. Trendy, fun, and modern, she'd always loved having three pretty, stylish daughters with cool, boyish names. But of course I kept my mouth shut. And, as per Mom's instructions, I'm planning on keeping it shut for the rest of July. *So go ahead, Mrs. P — call me Daniella all you want. See if I care.*

The plane floats down a few metres, taking my stomach with it. I wince from the stabbing pain in my ears and look around to see where my candy is. "Try yawning," Kat says. "It'll help."

I shake my head. "I can't yawn if I'm not tired."

"Try it anyway. It'll activate the muscles that open your eustachian tubes." She says it like I know what that means. Gotta love Kat.

"Thanks, but I'm way too psyched to yawn."

Before I can argue any more, she opens her mouth wide and lets out a loud, yodelling yawn, knowing full well I won't be able to stop myself now. "Gotcha, right?" she says when she's done, a devious grin spreading over her face. Sure enough, a second later I'm yawning too, so wide and long it's like I haven't slept in days. Miraculously, my ears open back up.

"You're awesome," I say. She takes my hand and gives it a squeeze. I smile and squeeze back. And then the two of us have one of those weird, psychic moments that happen sometimes. You know, like when you're thinking of a Taylor Swift song and then it comes on the radio a split second later?

"I'm so excited," we say at the same time. I giggle and whisper, "Jinx!" like I did when I was ten. Kat's eyes widen. Before I know what's happening, she leans forward and touches the bright red maple leaf embroidered into the fabric of the seat in front of us. Then she sighs and relaxes back into her chair. Beside us, Mrs. P nods her approval as she pats her daughter's hand. "Bravo, Katerina," she murmurs softly.

I stare at Kat in surprise, the giggle dead on my lips. "What are you doing?"

She glances shyly at me, her face slowly turning a warm shade of pink. "Sorry, old Greek habit. Touching red keeps away the bad luck."

"Really?" I wait for her to tell me she's just kidding.

She doesn't.

"So is everyone in Greece as superstitious as you two?" I ask.

Kat checks to see if her mother's listening, then leans close to whisper in my ear. "Actually, I'm not really superstitious; it's just Mummy who's into all this stuff. But she gets upset if I don't go along with it."

"Like with the bracelet?" I whisper back, glancing down at the chain of small blue eyeball beads snaking around Kat's thin wrist — a perfect match for the one her mother's wearing. I first noticed them this morning on the way to the airport.

"Mummy bought them for our trip," she explained, raising her arm to give me a better look. "They're *Mati* charms. She thinks they ward off evil spirits."

I pick up her wrist now and take a closer look at the bracelet. My insides twist at the sight of all those funny-looking little eyes staring back at me. "Evil spirits and touching red to keep bad luck away?" I whisper. "How can your mother believe that stuff?"

"It's just a Greek thing," she says. "Didn't I ever tell you the story about how she spat on me three times the day I turned thirteen? To keep the bad luck away, of course. And whatever you do, don't freak out when you see the bat bones she carries around in her purse."

I stare at her in shock, trying to figure out if she's joking or not. Sometimes with Kat it's hard to tell. "Bat bones? Really?"

She laughs and pulls her sleeve down to cover the eyeball bracelet. "Don't worry about it — we're going to have a great time. My aunt and uncle's resort is the nicest on the whole island. Sun and beaches and ocean as far as you can see. Just one more quick flight and then we'll be there."

My stomach flip-flops with excitement. I've never been to an actual beach before (the painted concrete shore at the wave pool isn't the same as the real thing). I smile and turn towards the window to watch the landing. In all the commotion of the past few minutes, I almost missed it. My heart jumps into my throat as the wheels hit the runway with a screeching jolt. I bounce up and down in my seat as the plane skitters to a stop.

We're in Greece. And it's going to be a summer to remember. I can feel it on my skin and in my bones — like that whispery tickle up your spine when something big's about to happen.

Yeah.

Chapter 2
• • • • • •

When we walk out of the airport, the first thing I notice is the air. It smells salty — like a bag of potato chips in my face. And hot like sauce. The sun is so strong, it crackles on my skin. I reach into my bag for a bottle of water. I've only been here a few minutes, but I'm thirsty already. I wait in the shade with Kat while Mrs. P gets us a taxi. A few minutes later, we're in the back seat of a dirty blue cab that's puttering away up a long pitted road. The road bends and curves around the base of a mountain. Actually, from what I can tell, there are mountains everywhere. Their craggy peaks rise up in every direction, surrounding us like an army of giants. Silver olive trees line the road for most of the ride. We bump along past boxy houses, bleached white like seashells; dry, rocky fields where herds of goats stand with bored, droopy eyes; and still more olive trees. At one point, we pass through a small village. I drink in the sights, trying to remember all the details for my journal. Wrinkled old grandpas sipping coffee and playing backgammon outside the cafés. Stray cats dozing in the sunshine on every street corner. Crowded laundry lines stringing all the pretty white houses together like pearls on a necklace. And, in between the houses and buildings, quick flashes of the ocean. Bright silver water against tall blue sky. I can't wait to see it up close!

We get to the resort just after six o'clock in the evening. Even though it's been a long day of travelling, I feel a burst of excited energy at the sight of it. Sitting at the very end of a long dirt road, the Olympic Palace is a whitewashed building with turquoise painted doors and matching shutters framing every window. Bright bougainvillea bushes in pink and purple grow from the rooftops and tumble down the white walls in a waterfall of colour.

A full-figured woman wearing a flower-printed summer dress and flip-flops is standing on the porch with one hand on her round hip and the other raised to her forehead, shielding her eyes from the glare of the sun. Beside her stands a short, fat man with a salt-and-pepper moustache. I giggle as we get closer and see that he's only wearing a bathing suit and a Blue Jays baseball cap. His round belly balloons out from his waist like a hairy, overgrown watermelon. Kat rolls down the window and waves.

"Thea Sophia! Theo John! We're here!"

With arms outstretched, the pair hurries towards our taxi as it bounds up the gravel driveway. They pull Kat and her mother from the car and hug them so hard, I worry they might suffocate. I creep out of the cab and stand off to the side, watching the reunion from a distance. The heat's so thick, I can feel it in my throat. When they're done hugging, the aunt and uncle spot me and run over as quickly as their round bodies will allow. The woman catches my face between her hands and kisses my cheeks three times.

"*Ti kanis*, Dani. How are you? Any friend of Katerina is welcome here — like family!"

I smile. "Thanks, Mrs. Karras."

"No. Please, call me Sophia. And he's John," she adds, ges-turing towards her husband with an outstretched thumb. "*Ella* — come! We're planning a big dinner tonight in your honour. But first you'll need to rest. Let me show you to your room."

Kat's uncle John might be fat, but he's as strong as an ox. He hefts a suitcase up under each arm and then reaches down and pulls up another in each hand. With a grin spreading under his moustache, he leads us to our room. It's spacious and bright with walls, like the rest of the building, painted a pure, snowy white — a colour, Kat explains, that helps to keep the place cool. There's a dresser, a couple of chairs, a TV, and two double beds covered with thin blankets of a bright coral pink colour that makes me think of the inside of a conch shell. John places the suitcases on a rack at the foot of each bed and, with a final round of hugs, leaves us to freshen up.

After twelve hours of travelling, my body's completely lost track of what time of day it is back home in Toronto. I'm tired and nauseous and grimy and hungry. The small island plane flew at a really low altitude, and the ride was so bumpy I thought I was going to hurl up my airplane-portioned, microwave-reheated *moussaka* the entire time we were in the air.

But despite all this, resting is the last thing on my mind. I'm itching to go exploring. Kat, however, is another story. As soon as John's gone, she kicks off her sandals and belly-flops onto the nearest bed. Mrs. Papadakis immediately begins unpacking her daughter's bags, clucking under her breath in Greek.

"*Cardia mou, louloudi mou* — a nice nap before dinner is exactly what you need."

Well, I'm tired too. But as exhausted as I feel, I know I can't rest until I see the ocean up close. My whole body is buzzing with anticipation. Heading over to the window, I fling open the curtains. The bubble of excitement in my chest deflates a bit when I see the grey, concrete parking lot staring back at me. Suddenly I understand exactly why this room was given to us for free. Undaunted, I march over to Kat's side, take her by the hand, and yank her up off the mattress.

"Come on, we can sleep later. Let's go see the beach."

She groans and flops like a skinny, overcooked spaghetti noodle. Mrs. P marches over and shoos me away. "Stop, Daniella. She needs her rest. And you do too."

Dodging her flapping hands, I yank on Kat again, harder this time. "Come on, please. Just for a bit before it gets dark."

I manage to pull her halfway off the bed before she finally rises to her feet. "All right, all right," she groans, "but just for a few minutes."

Her eyelids droop with exhaustion, but I don't care. The beach is calling my name. Happy-clapping, I skip out of the room. "We'll be back soon, Mrs. P!"

When we reach the end of the hallway, Kat pushes open a rounded door and we step outside into a courtyard bordered with flower beds and life-sized marble statues of ancient toga-clad gods and goddesses. Their bodies and faces have been sculpted so beautifully, they remind me of those perfect-looking models on the covers of the romance novels Kat's always reading. She's obsessed with those books, although she told me once that her mother doesn't approve. Back in Toronto, she has a whole stack hidden away at the back of her closet where Mrs. P can't find them and confiscate them. And she's always spending her allowance on more books to add to her collection. One time I asked Kat why a smart girl like her doesn't read anything but love stories. Her cheeks turned pink and she said, "Guess I'm just a born romantic." I told her not to be embarrassed and that I like a good love story just as much as the next person. To be honest, it probably made me like her even more. Like we finally had something in common. But just between you and me, I wonder where's she going to hide those books now that we're all sharing a room.

"Okay, which way to the beach?" I ask, trying to see past the statues. That's when I hear it — the soft roar of the waves breaking over sand. Kat points to a narrow path leading away from the trees at the far end of the courtyard.

"That's the shortcut to the water. There's a natural stairway built out of the rock."

As I soon discover, calling it a "stairway" is generous. "Lawsuit-waiting-to-happen" would be a better description. "Isn't there an easier way down?" I ask, trying to keep my balance on the slippery pile of stones beneath my feet.

Kat nods, bounding ahead of me like a mountain goat. "There's a paved road, but it takes a lot longer."

After another minute, we make it down unscathed. Now that I'm not focusing on survival anymore, I can finally take my eyes off the rocks and look around. The instant I see the water, my breath flies out with a sharp gasp. I've never seen water that shade of blue in my life. It's like the sky tipped over and spilled itself at our feet. Under the warmth of the sun, the surface glitters and sparkles like a field of sapphires. And the sand is powdery and white and perfect. The sun's still high enough to reflect off the surface and heat up my skin. Fanning my sweaty face with my hands, I squint into the light and gaze out towards the water like a thirsty wanderer aching for a drink.

"Let's go, Kat!" I say, flicking off my shoes so I can feel the sand between my toes.

We weave our way in and around the maze of outstretched bodies. The closer we get, the more eager I am to feel that blue water on my skin. After a minute, I break into a run. With my clothes still on, I splash a few metres into the surf then dive into a breaking wave. The water feels as fantastic as it looks. It's warm and soft and gentle — like a perfect kiss. Salt tickles my throat and stings the corners of my eyes as I come up for air. I flip around onto my back, stretch my arms out above my head, and stare up at the cloudless sky — so pure and clear and blue, it seems to go on forever. It's like heaven. And I want to share it with somebody. Standing up, I wave for Kat to come join me. She's too far away for me to hear her reply, but I see her laughing and shaking her head. *Okay, suit yourself.*

After about ten minutes of floating I'm satisfied. I turn around and head back to the shore. My shorts and T-shirt stick to me like a fresh coat of paint as I emerge from the sea. A pair of cute bathing-suit–clad boys stop and smile.

"Water's awesome!" I say, waving as I pass them, not knowing or caring if they speak English. Kat runs over to me, her dark brown eyes awake again. The fresh sea air must have revived her.

"Oh my God! You're crazy!"

I twist my hair into a long brown rope and squeeze out a stream of salt water. "You're the crazy one. That water's amazing."

Kat takes a step back while I shake the water off my hands. "Thanks, but I prefer to use my bathing suit. And besides, we've got all month to swim."

"Yeah, and I plan on diving in every chance I get. Life's too short to stand on the sidelines."

Kat just stares at me like we're from completely different planets. And I guess in some ways, we kind of are. To be honest, a part of me is still kind of surprised that we're on this trip together. I mean, who could ever have imagined that me and my math tutor would become such good friends? When Kat first transferred to our school last September, I guessed from her granny glasses and plain-looking clothes that she was more interested in work than fun. You know the type — one of those snobby, brainiac kids who always know the answer to every teacher's question. But I obviously didn't know the real Kat ... yet. That changed after the winter report cards came back. Once my parents found out that I was failing math, they hired the smartest kid in school to be my tutor. And that kid was Kat.

We started spending every afternoon studying together. Once I got to know her, I realized I was totally wrong. She wasn't a snob at all — just shy and a bit quiet. After a couple of weeks went by, she opened herself up to me like a Christmas present. That's when I found out she wasn't just the smartest kid in school, she was also one of the funniest. She could keep me laughing for hours with her impersonations of our teachers. And she never made me feel dumb because I didn't understand math. In fact, after my lessons with her I'd actually feel kind of smart. Nobody's ever made me feel like that. Definitely a first for me.

Sometimes she'll get this sad look in her eyes. Totally out of the blue. And no matter what I say or do, it won't go away. When that happens, it makes me a little sad too. And then I start to worry that maybe I'm not being a good enough friend. I wish I knew how to fix that.

I squeal at the sting of salt water dripping into my eyes. Just then, an older boy wearing a white waiter's apron jogs over from the hotel's waterside café and hands me a towel. I take it gratefully. "That's sweet. Thanks."

I don't know if he understands me or not because he doesn't reply. He just nods and watches as I wipe off my dripping face. When he steps forward as if to offer his assistance with the rest of me, Kat makes a funny noise under her breath and takes me by the arm — a bit more firmly than necessary.

"Come on, Dani. We better get back before Mummy comes looking for us. Dinner's in half an hour."

With a smile, I hand the waiter back his towel and follow Kat back up the rock "stairs." By the time we make it back to our room, the light from the day's beginning to fade. Mrs. P sucks lemons again the second she sees me. Her coal black eyes slide over my dripping hair and clothes, oozing disapproval. She doesn't say anything, but her thoughts are as clear as the ocean water puddling around my feet.

I do my best to ignore her.

Chapter 3
• • • • • •

After a quick shower to wash away the salt water and sand, I comb my long hair back into a wet ponytail and focus on wardrobe options. After a bunch of false starts, I try on one of the three new sundresses I bought especially for Greece. *Yup — just right for a warm summer night*, I think, admiring my reflection in the mirror.

When I come out of the bathroom, I see that Kat had the same sundress idea. Except hers looks like it's a vintage edition straight out of the '90s. And it's painfully obvious that she doesn't even come close to filling it out. I shoot her an encouraging smile.

"Wow, you look beautiful, Kat."

"Ptoo-ptoo-ptoo," Mrs. P mutters, raising a tissue to her mouth.

I stare at her in surprise.

Yeah, she totally just spat.

Kat shrugs her bony shoulders and flashes her braces at me. Poor Kat. She's still desperately praying for a visit from the boob fairy. The only girl in our grade who doesn't wear a bra yet. Thank God, I was able to convince her to trade those granny glasses of hers for contact lenses before our trip. Now at least she's got a chance at snagging a boyfriend this summer. If her mom ever lets her out of her sight, that is. Last month, Kat confided to me that she'd never been on a date before. "My mother doesn't let me yet," she said. We were at the library, studying for the final math exam when she told me.

"Okay, but you've been kissed, right?" I asked.

She just shook her head.

"Not even once?"

She frowned and crossed her arms in front of her skinny chest. "No. Is that really bad?"

Because I could see she was already embarrassed about it, I tried to be cool so she wouldn't feel any worse. "No, it's not *bad*. Lots of people have never been kissed. But it's something we can work on changing. Like, soon."

"Soon?" She was turning red just talking about it. And her eyes were wide with panic. Suddenly, I felt a protective, big-sisterly kind of feeling rise up in my chest — which was weird since Kat was older by a couple of months. But at that moment, she looked way more like a frightened little kid than a teenager with the highest grade point average in the entire eighth grade class. Leaning across the desk, I put my arm around her shoulders and gave her an encouraging squish.

"Yeah, soon. Romance isn't just for books, you know. You're almost *fourteen*, dude. Believe me, you don't want to wait any longer. Once you've been kissed, everything changes."

"Everything?"

I could practically hear her teeth chattering with fear. "Yeah, but don't worry. It's kind of like magic. For starters, you won't feel like a little kid anymore. And once it happens, you'll start to see the world a bit differently. And, believe it or not, people will see a difference in you too."

Kat tried to force a smile, but I knew she was still scared. Heck, I could almost see her terrified heart pounding through her T-shirt. Right then and there, I decided to make it my mission for the summer. I was going to make sure Kat snuck in a little romance on this trip. And not just from one of her books.

"Come, girls, we don't want to keep my sister waiting," Mrs. P says. With her hands flapping like a frantic chicken, she corrals us out of the hotel room. This time, I have no urge to argue with her. The swim must have refreshed me from a day of travel because I'm suddenly hungry for my first real meal of the trip. Since it's getting dark, we avoid the rocky cliff and take the longer, smoother route down to the beach. When we get there, the Karrases are waiting for us at the same waterside café we saw earlier. Sophia rises to her feet and waves us over to a table just on the edge of the sand.

"*Kalos orisate*, welcome to our little restaurant. I hope you brought good appetites!"

The table's covered in a soft, blue cloth and illuminated by dozens of tiny votive candles. The light breeze that wafts in off the water makes the flames flicker like a swarm of dancing fireflies. A plate of slick, black olives sits in the middle of the table next to a larger plate of tomatoes and a brick of porous feta cheese. Suddenly hungry, I pull up a chair. There's a mewling army of cats winding their skinny bodies in and out of the table legs. *Do they belong to the hotel?* While I take a seat next to the sand, Kat and her mother go to hug a young woman with long black hair who's standing behind John's chair. Before I have a chance to ask who she is, Sophia introduces us.

"Dani, this is my daughter, Thalia. She's come home for her summer vacation from the University of Athens."

"Hi, nice to meet you," I say, reaching my right hand out to shake hers. At the same time, I reach my foot out from under the table and dig my toes in the soft sand. The beach is that irresistible to me. I can't sit so close and not touch it. A moment later, there's a tap on my shoulder and a deep, honeyed voice crooning in my ear.

"I see you're all dry now. Are you planning another swim, or are you done for the day?"

I twist around to see the same waiter who offered me the towel earlier that evening. *So he does speak English.* "Oh, hi. No, I'm done. Thanks."

He lingers for another few seconds, drinking me up with his dark eyes. As soon as he's gone, Thalia sits down in the seat beside mine and whispers in my ear. "That's Costa. Watch out for him. He has big eyes for beautiful girls."

Turning my head, I see him stacking dishes by the kitchen door. As if sensing my gaze, he looks back at me, raises one eyebrow, and winks. I don't want to encourage him, so I swallow my usual smile and pop an olive into my mouth instead. He's cute, but I can't help feeling creeped out by his age. He's probably seventeen or eighteen — way too old to be flirting with me. And anyway, I'm not looking for romance right now. Just before leaving Toronto, I pulled the plug on my two-month relationship with Alec Soto, the captain of our school's hockey team. He was my first boyfriend, and when we started hanging out I thought he was, like, Prince Charming or something. But those two months weren't exactly a fairy tale. It didn't take long for me to figure out that he was just a tall, oversized ego on ice skates. Needless to say, I'm happy to take a few weeks off from boys. As far as I'm concerned, any romance this summer is going to be for Kat.

When we're ready to start the meal, Mrs. P takes a seat next to her brother-in-law and Kat pulls up the chair on the other side of me. Sitting at the head of the table, Sophia claps her hands to get our attention.

"Tonight, we're here to celebrate our daughter who's come home for another summer and our guests who've come all the way from Toronto to be with us on our little island. Reuniting with friends and family is the food that nourishes our souls. Now, let us nourish our bodies and introduce our Canadian friend Dani to some authentic Greek cooking."

I spread my napkin across my lap, excited to taste some new food. That is, until Costa arrives at the table carrying a large platter of deep-fried tarantulas. Trying to control my gag reflex, I quickly pass the plate to Kat. She takes a heaping portion and tries to pass it back to me. "Come on, it's squid — *calamari*. You must have tasted this before at home."

I fold my arms across my chest and shake my head. "Yeah, but it always comes in nice neat circles. Not these spidery-looking things."

She scoops one off the platter and puts it on my plate. "Those are just the tentacles. Try it. You'll love it!"

After another minute of urging, I agree to try one. The first bite's crunchy and the rest of it melts deliciously between my teeth. *Maybe this authentic Greek cooking isn't going to be so bad after all.* Next come the *dolmades* — rice-stuffed vine leaves — which don't faze me a bit. After the squid tentacles, I'm ready to try anything. Then a plate of *taramosalata* — fish eggs with potato. After that, some *saganaki* — which means, *thank you God*, fried cheese. Every time Costa arrives with a new platter of food, he always makes a big point to serve me first. I pretend not to notice.

For the final course, we're all invited to choose our own fish from the seafood locker at the back of the restaurant. The daily catch is lying there on a bed of ice, their dead eyes bulging out of their heads. For the second time that night, I feel like gagging. Averting my eyes from the locker, I tap Kat on the shoulder. "Can you help me out? I don't know how to choose a fish."

When she turns around, she's all bulging eyes and sucked-in cheeks and sticking-out lips. The perfect fish face.

"Be serious," I laugh, swatting her arm.

"Okay, relax. It's easy. Just poke the side. If your finger leaves a dent in the skin, then the fish isn't fresh."

Overhearing us, Thalia comes up behind us and wags her finger at her younger cousin. "Hey, what are you talking about? The fish is always fresh at our hotel. Right?"

Kat turns a bright shade of pink. "Right. Of course it is. Sorry."

Since I don't want to touch one of those slimy fish anyway, I decide to take Thalia's word for it and point to the plump, silvery one in front of me. The chef picks it up and begins to prep it for the grill. Like everything else I've eaten that night, it turns out to be delicious. When the meal's over, Costa starts clearing away the dishes. That's when I notice a few things missing on his right hand. I manage to swallow my startled scream. But the look on my face betrays my shock.

"Costa!" Sophia calls out. "I think it's time to tell our Dani the story of how you lost those fingers."

He grins, his teeth glowing white against his dark, tanned skin. "Fine, but only over a glass of ouzo. That's my price."

Jogging back to the kitchen, Costa comes back with a tray of small glasses and a bottle. He gives each of us a glass, telling the story while he fills each one with the watery liquid from the bottle.

"My father was a fisherman and I grew up on the sea. When I was fourteen, times got hard for my father and he lost his boat to his creditors. After a few weeks with no income, he heard about a way to catch fish without a boat. All you had to do was throw a stick of dynamite in the water and scoop up the dead fish with a net when they floated to the surface. We did that for about a year until the dynamite went off too early — in my hand. The day I lost my fingers was the day my father gave up fishing by dynamite and I gave up fishing altogether. Now I wait tables. A much less dangerous profession. And I use my lines to catch girls instead of fish."

The table erupts with laughter, and I can tell from the easy smile on Costa's face that he enjoys having an appreciative audience. When all the glasses are filled, he pulls up a chair beside Sophia and joins us at the table. Pointing to my glass, I nudge Thalia with my elbow.

"What did he say this is?"

"Ouzo. It's anise-flavoured liqueur."

It takes me a moment to understand what that means. *Alcohol?* My mother's words of warning begin echoing in my head again. Is Mrs. P going to report me if I have a drink on my very first night? With a glance at my chaperone, I shake my head and push the glass away. "Sorry, but I'm not nineteen yet."

When Thalia bursts out laughing, Kat leans over and whispers in my ear. "You're in Greece now. It's okay to have a sip at a private party."

I stare at her in surprise for a few seconds. Then my eyes swing around the table to find my chaperone. "Really? Is that true, Mrs. Papadakis?"

She nods and reaches for her own glass. "Go ahead, Daniella. But be careful. It's a bit strong if you aren't used to it."

I pick up my ouzo and give it a sniff; the powerful smell of black licorice fills my nose. Before I can take a taste, Sophia stands up and raises her glass in the air.

"*Stin ygia mas* — to our health. *Opa!*"

"*Opa!*" the rest of us echo.

I raise the glass to my lips and take a gulp. The ouzo explodes in my mouth like a ball of fire on my tongue. For a crazy moment, I actually think Costa might have put one of those sticks of dynamite in my glass. I spit it out onto the table, scream, and reach for some water to douse the burning in my throat. That's the moment we finally hear from John, who hasn't said a single word all night. A big, booming chuckle flies out from under that bushy moustache, rattling his huge stomach until he begins to shake like a jolly Mediterranean Santa Claus. A moment later, Mrs. P joins in. She shrieks and cackles so hard, she actually drowns out John's mighty laugh. I stare at her in shock. *Wow, maybe she's not such a sourpuss after all.* Temporarily forgetting the awful taste of the ouzo, I begin to laugh too. But I stop when I see Costa watching me from across the table. His eyes stick to me like sand to a wet bathing suit.

When he winks, the burn in my throat goes cold.

Chapter 4

• • • • • •

Dear Mom, yesterday I learned all about traditional Greek food and beverages and fishing techniques. Today, Kat and I plan on studying local beach life in its natural habitat ...

Okay, so Greece is totally, incredibly epic. Like teenage nirvana. Our island has to be the nicest place I've ever seen in my life. It's made up of a ring of craggy mountains, the tallest of which spring up from the centre of the island like a giant, sticking-out nose. If you look beyond the parking lot, the window in our room has a great view of that mountain and the monastery that sits on the top. But I'm never in our room long enough to look at the view. Kat and I are spending every moment possible at the beach. Even though I've been told that the resort has a pool, the whole week we've been here I haven't even seen it. Guess I'm just not a pool kind of gal. I much prefer the feel of soft sand between my toes to concrete, the taste of salt water to chlorine, and a view of the ocean to a diving board. Thankfully, Kat feels the same way as me.

There's a perfect spot right by the water that we reserve with our towels every morning before breakfast. We spend all day swimming, suntanning, napping in the shade, and snacking on pita and *tzatziki* beside the ocean. Every day I bring my journal and my iPod to keep me busy and Kat brings her contraband romance novels and reads them when her mom's not looking.

Another one of our favourite pastimes is watching the cute boys strutting around the beach. Because hotel guests are coming and going all the time, there's always a fresh selection — kind of like the fish in the seafood locker at the waterside café. I'm crossing my fingers that Kat will start talking with one of them soon. With a mother like Mrs. P, she definitely needs a bit of fun in her life. And believe me, I'm doing my best to help her find the right guy. But choosing a boy for Kat's first kiss isn't as easy as you might think. Anyone too good-looking or confident immediately gets my veto. A boy like that will probably scare her away faster than Mrs. P can chase them off. No, someone cute and nice and young would be perfect. Maybe even a bit shy, like her. Every day, I scan the beach for potential candidates for my friend. I'm on a mission. More than anything, I want Kat to get her nose out of those books so she can find some romance in real life.

"How 'bout that one?" I hear myself saying at least fifteen times every day.

Or: "He looks nice ..."

Or: "What do you think of that guy over there?"

But Kat's either incredibly picky or incredibly petrified because she keeps finding reason after reason not to go up and talk to any of them. *Too muscled ... too skinny ... too short ... too tall ... too much swagger.* Sometimes, when they're out of sight, she'll jump to her feet and do a silly, exaggerated impersonation of them that always gets us giggling. But so far, I'm striking out big time. Still, I'm not ready to give up on Kat yet. We have over two weeks left of our trip — plenty of time to find her someone great.

On those rare occasions when we feel like getting off the beach, there're bikes for us to use to explore the area. And Sophia and John are fantastic at making sure we have everything we want.

Feel like going snorkelling? Great, we'll charter a boat for the day.

In the mood to go shopping? We'll rent you a couple of scooters.

Want to see more of the island? We'll arrange for donkey rides up to the top of the mountain.

That last one turns out to be the best. On our eighth day, Kat and I wake up early to go for a donkey ride up to the ancient monastery at the very top. Of course, Mrs. Papadakis comes along too. The ride up is a bit scary because the route's steep and the donkeys are sweaty and probably not too happy to be lugging us up that big mountain. But the long, hot climb is definitely worth it. At the top we're greeted with beautiful gardens, smiling priests, and a breathtaking view of the island and the surrounding sea. The sky above us is like a work of art — so clear and blue I feel like I could reach out and touch it. And the sunlight shimmers over everything like a halo. It's all so beautiful, I can't stop taking pictures.

"I never see any clouds in the sky here. Where are they all?" I ask Mrs. P as I click away on my camera.

"Clouds? They usually only come in winter."

I realize right then and there why those holy men put their home at the highest point — it probably makes them feel like they're living in heaven up there in the infinite blue sky. Even for an atheist like me, it's pretty inspiring. I wave at Kat to come take my picture so I have something to show my parents when I get back to Toronto. I make her take a photo of me in front of the monastery, so my parents will think I was behaving my-self. And then another photo in front of some important-looking old building, so my parents will think I cared about Greek history. I take the camera back so I can take some shots of her. "Smile, Kat," I say, because out of nowhere that sad look of hers is back again. "Come on, Kat. For me?" I beg. She smiles, but it doesn't quite reach her eyes.

Before we leave the monastery, Kat and Mrs. P insist on kiss-ing the priest's hand. They try to convince me to do it also. "Come on, he'll give you a blessing," Kat whispers, pulling my arm as we approach the black-robed priest. Smiling broadly through his flowing ash-coloured beard, he extends his hand towards us.

"No, thanks," I mumble. Although he seems friendly enough, my whole body itches with discomfort just looking at him. While the others kneel to kiss his hand, I turn and hurry away. It feels too much like another one of those superstitions.

On the way down the mountain, my mood darkens when I ask Kat if she wants to check out the local discos later that night. The path is now wide enough for us to ride side by side, with Mrs. P trailing behind.

"There was a boy at the beach talking about one club in particular yesterday. It sounds like a blast."

"I don't know ..."

"Come on. I'll put some makeup on you. And we can go on the scooters. Maybe find a cute boy for you there?"

She fiddles with the shaggy strands on her donkey's mane. "Um, I don't think my mom would like it."

I roll my eyes. Mrs. P could probably suck the fun out of a circus clown. "Do we have to tell her? Come on, Kat, it's time to stop reading books about romance and start living it. Your mother doesn't have to know everything we do."

Kat lowers her voice to a whisper. "You mean sneak out? How on earth would we pull that off?"

My heart drops into my stomach. Kat kind of has a point. Because the three of us share a room, it'll probably be hard. I glance back and see Mrs. Papadakis watching me from on top of her donkey. Out of nowhere, I begin to feel nauseous. I can't figure out if it's because of the musky smell from the overheated donkey or the slow, rocking gait of the ride or my chaperone's eyes boring into me. When I turn forward again, I can still feel her eyes on my back.

How does Kat manage? Mrs. P is such a downer. It's like she wants Kat to live like one of these priests in their sheltered monastery. What if Kat meets a cute boy? There'll be zero chance for any privacy.

Beside me, her donkey lets out a loud, trumpeting fart. She starts to laugh, and normally I would too if I weren't so pissed off and queasy. As soon as we get back from the donkey ride, I pull the hotel phone into the closet and call my mom. It only takes her a second to detect the pout in my voice.

"What's wrong, Dani? Is Mrs. Papadakis taking good care of you?"

I snort. "Too good. She's *always* watching us!"

From an ocean away, Mom's laugh brushes my ear. "Isn't that what a chaperone is for?" she asks.

"Seriously, Mom. It's suffocating."

I hear a long sigh on the other end of the line. "Honey, listen. You're thirteen years old and a long way from home. Your sisters were both much older before Dad and I allowed them to go away without us. The only reason we agreed to this trip is because we knew that Mrs. Papadakis would keep an eye on you. I guess if you really don't like it, you can always come back early."

"Fine, maybe I will."

"Should I call the travel agent, then?" she asks. But I can tell from the smile in her voice that she's not taking my threat very seriously. And that turns out to be a good thing. Because the very next day, I meet Nick.

Yeah.

Chapter 5
• • • • • •

When I see him striding up the beach towards our towels, I actually stop breathing. He's tall and thin, but muscular, not skinny. And the way he wears his bathing suit makes my breath flutter in my throat.

The way a boy looks in a bathing suit is of supreme importance. It can't be too tight or too loose, too long or too short. And obviously, a Speedo is a complete deal-breaker. The way a boy walks in his bathing suit is really important too.

Does he saunter casually? Then he's probably an easygoing jock.

Does he cover himself with tanning oil and strut? Jerk alert!

Does he stick his hands in his pockets, shuffle, and search the shore for seashells? Cringe-worthy! Run the other way!

If a boy can't wear a bathing suit decently, chances are he probably won't kiss well either. I know because I overheard my two older sisters talking about it last summer. For reasons that I don't really understand, it seems there's a mysterious but undeniable connection between these two things.

But at the moment, the boy who's heading towards us is wearing his bathing suit perfectly. He's smiling as he saunters through the sand; as he gets closer I can see that he's a little bow-legged. Adorable! He's easily the cutest boy I've seen all summer.

"What about this one, Kat?" I whisper. But as soon as the words are out of my mouth, I want to pull them back in. All my good intentions for Kat fly away in an uncontrollable burst of selfishness. With my heart drumming painfully against my ribs, I realize that this is one boy I want for myself. Ignoring the protest of my guilty conscience, I push my hair back behind my ears, take my sunglasses off, and wait for him to notice me. Imagine my shock when he walks right past me straight to Kat and sweeps her up into a big hug.

She shrieks with happiness. I sit there trying to figure out what the heck is going on. *These two know each other? Oh please, please, PLEASE let them be cousins or step-siblings or something related like that.*

"What are you doing here?" Kat squeals, twirling around in his arms. "I didn't know you were coming to Greece this summer!"

Mr. Perfect Bathing Suit grins and deposits her gently back down on the sand.

"My parents decided to send me at the last minute. I guess being a camp counsellor wasn't my thing because I only survived one week in that place before I had to get out of there. I hitched a ride home last Friday." He cocks his head to the side. "Hey, did you get contact lenses? You look great."

"Forget about that — what do you mean, you hitchhiked?" Kat gasps while I stand back and admire this guy's looks. His skin is smooth and olive-toned, like Kat's. His lips are full and turned up at the corners — even as he complains about camp, he seems to be smiling. His nose makes a perfectly straight line from top to bottom while his hair is a mop of thick, unruly chestnut curls. My fingers itch to run through them and sort them out curl by curl.

"Hitchhiking's really dangerous," Kat says. "You could have been kidnapped."

Wow, that's so something Mrs. P would say, I think. I adjust the straps on my bathing suit and smooth back my hair, waiting for my introduction.

"I don't care. I had to get out of there," he replies. "Trust me, you'd have done the same. The camp was lame — swarms of mosquitoes, bratty kids, damp mouldy cabins, bug-infested mattresses. So Mom called Sophia and John and asked if I could come to Greece. She put me on a plane the next day. I'm supposed to go back home to Toronto with you and your mom at the end of the month."

See, he's talking like he's part of the family. They must be cousins, right? Yeah, I'm totally in the clear.

"Anyway," he continues, "I thought I could hang out with you for the next few weeks. But I didn't know you were here with a friend …"

Finally, Mr. Perfect Bathing Suit looks my way. He has long eyelashes and these incredible green eyes with tiny flecks of gold that reflect the light of the sun. I smile my signature smile. He blushes and quickly looks down at his feet.

Shy *and* cute? Sweet! I could die right then and there. It's time for me to interrupt this conversation. I step forward and hold out my hand. "Hi, I'm Dani."

Kat slaps the side of her head. "Oops. I'm sorry. Nick Barbas, this is my friend Dani Price from Toronto. She's vacationing with me and Mummy."

Nick takes my hand and gives it a gentle shake. The skin on his palm is rough and a bit calloused. I take another small step closer. "Why didn't you tell me you had a cousin, Kat?"

She laughs and shakes her head. "We're not cousins. But our families are so close, it's kind of like we're related. Nick's parents and mine are friends from the old days when they all lived here in Greece. We've known each other since we were babies."

Not wanting to break our connection so soon, I let my fingers linger in Nick's a moment longer. My skin feels electric against his, like there's a current of energy running between us. With my free hand, I point to the spot beside my towel. "Sorry to hear your summer plans got squashed. Come and join us, if you want. There's loads of room. And no mosquitoes."

He smiles at my joke, and I feel like I'm going to melt into a puddle at his feet. The three of us spend the rest of the afternoon together. *He's the one,* I think, waving goodbye as he saunters back to his room. The instant he's out of sight, I turn to Kat and grab onto her twiggy arm.

"I need deets. How old is he?"

"He just turned fourteen."

"And you said you guys are 'like family,' right?"

She nods. Her brown eyes search my blue ones, trying to read the thoughts behind them. "Yeah, why?" The question marks in her voice stretch out long and slow over the sand.

"Well, I was just thinking that if you and Nick are like family, then you won't mind if I go for him?"

"Go for *Nick*?" she echoes, twisting uncomfortably on her towel. It looks like she's trying to dislodge a shell from her butt. "No, um, I guess I don't mind."

She isn't doing a great job of convincing me. "Really?" I press, giving her arm a shake. "Are you positive? I won't if you tell me you like him. Because this summer is supposed to be about finding a boy for you, right?"

She twists some more. "No, go ahead ... I ... I guess it's just strange for me to think of him that way. You know?"

"So, you're sure? You don't mind?" Leaning a bit closer, I peer at her face, trying to decipher that strange knot in the middle of her forehead. *Is she telling the truth? Is she really okay with this?* "I'll still help you find someone. I promise. And when that happens, we can even double date. How much fun would that be, right? Trust me, your first kiss is totally happening this summer."

She stops twisting and nods, and then she gives me a weak smile. When the knot in her forehead vanishes, my heart gives a leap of joy. I throw my arms around her bony shoulders and hug her tight. "Thanks, Kat!"

But just between you and me, there's a tiny hole leaking air out of my happiness balloon. I'm worried I'm not being a good enough friend for Kat.

I told you so, didn't I?

Why, you want to know.

Because deep down I'm worried that I'm not going to be able to make good on my promise — the one about finding her a boy to kiss. Because after meeting Nick I'm going to have a hard time looking at anyone else. Like, ever again.

Chapter 6
• • • • • •

The very next night is Thalia's birthday, and to celebrate, Sophia and John hired a local Greek band to play at the waterside café. All of the guests at the hotel are invited. Of course there's a ton of food and bottles of ouzo flowing. My mouth burns just at the smell of it. This time, I decide to keep my distance.

In between courses, everyone dances. At first when Kat invites me to Greek dance with her family, I say no. I'm too nervous about doing it wrong and looking silly. But she pulls on my arm until I think it's going to come out of its socket.

"Don't be that way. Come on, it's fun. I'll show you how."

Once I start, I'm surprised to find out that it isn't as hard as I thought it would be. Everyone basically just holds hands and hops around in a big circle to the rhythm of the music.

Eight steps forward, three steps back, eight steps forward, three steps back ...

I guess because she's the birthday girl, Thalia leads all the circle dances. She's laughing and waving a dinner napkin around with her free hand and looking like a princess in her white lace sundress. Nick knows how to Greek dance too. Every time we start a new round, he makes sure he's beside me holding my hand. Whenever I look up he's watching me with those gorgeous green eyes. It's pretty obvious that it's his way of announcing he's interested. Because I sense that he's shy, I decide to spare him my usual hard-to-get tricks and let him hold my hand. That current of energy is still going strong, buzzing between our fingers like a live wire. *Does he feel that too?* During the dances, sometimes one of the men will go into the middle of the circle and do a trick to show off for the women. John goes first, doing a funny move where he snaps his fingers and slaps his ankles as his big tummy bounces and bobs up and down to the music. That makes Sophia laugh so hard I think she'll have to stop dancing and sit down to catch her breath. Then Costa breaks into the middle and begins dancing around a small glass of ouzo with his arms outstretched and the fingers on his good hand snapping. After a couple of minutes, he kneels down in front of it, picks it up with his teeth, and drinks it without using his hands. When he's done, the entire café cheers. Costa beams with pride as he wipes the final drops of ouzo from his mouth.

It's a wild party, and the later the night gets, the crazier people act. When the meal's finally over, Thalia stands up and hurls her plate to the tiled floor. It smashes into a thousand tiny pieces.

She throws her head back and cries, "*Opa!*" at the top of her lungs.

One by one, everyone else in the café stands up and does the same. For the next few minutes, the air is filled with the brittle splash of crashing dinnerware. I've never seen anything like it in my life. Kat's standing beside me. She points at the plate in front of me and nudges me with her pointy elbow. "Go on, Dani. Break it," she says over the din.

I pick up the plate, weighing it in my hand. I have no idea why everyone is smashing them, but it looks like fun. I hesitate another second. "Are you sure?"

"Of course. It's tradition," she says, grinning. And that's all the encouragement I need. Lifting the plate high above my head, I fling it down to the floor at my feet and yell, "*Opa!*" It comes apart with a satisfying crash. Smithereens in every direction. How weirdly destructive. And how hugely satisfying at the same time. I feel giddy and lightheaded, even though I'm staying far away from the ouzo. As soon as the last plate is smashed, everyone rises to their feet and the dancing starts all over again. Although truthfully by this point, there's a lot more stumbling going on than dancing. Laughing and singing and hopping, we move around the dance floor in a rowdy circle, shards of broken dishes crunching beneath our shoes with every step. Nick's still beside me holding my hand, but I'm worried that my palms are getting sweaty and gross. After all this dancing, I'm beginning to overheat.

Just as I'm about to break away from the circle and try to cool off, Thalia freezes on the spot and lets out a sharp cry. Her voice rises above the music in a shriek of panic.

"*A crow!*"

The musicians stop playing, the guests stop dancing, and every-one turns to follow the direction of her trembling finger as it points across the restaurant. My eyes fly to the spot where the sand meets the blue tiles of the restaurant floor. There's a small black crow staring at the assembled party — claws hidden in the soft sand; greasy feathers reflecting the patio lights; and gleaming black eyes taking in the scene with cool interest.

Weird. What's a bird doing out so late at night? I wonder. *Scavenging for food?*

Before I can figure it out, Thalia takes a step towards the bird, waving it off with her hands. "*Sto kalo! Sto kalo!*" I hear her yell. The crow shakes its tail feathers, cocks its dark head to one side, and lets out a raspy *caw.* Fanning my burning face with my hands, I watch Thalia advance faster on the bird, charging at it like a bull. "*Sto kalo! Sto kalo!*" she screeches. This time, she manages to scare it off. With black wings unfolding like a sinister cloak, the crow turns, makes three quick hops towards the beach, and takes flight over the ocean. As it disappears into the night, I lean towards Kat and whisper, "Why is Thalia so upset? It's just a stupid bird."

When she turns to answer me, I see that her eyebrows are crunched up with worry. "Greeks believe that crows are omens of doom. She doesn't want bad luck to come to any of her guests."

Omens of doom? Okay, this superstition stuff is officially get-ting ridiculous. I fan my face a little harder as I try to think of a way to tell Kat that her family is crazy … without hurting her feelings, of course. Behind me, the band starts up the music again. Uh-uh ... no more dancing for me. It's time for a break.

"Well, omens of doom don't bother me. I'm going to get some air. Be back soon."

Desperate to cool off, I slip away from the crowd and make my way towards the ocean. I just need to dip my feet in the water and let the sea breeze blow over my damp, hot skin for a few minutes. I know that'll make me feel better. As I walk along the shore, the waves lap softly at my toes. I can't help thinking how nice it would feel to just jump in right then and there. Mrs. P would be *so* pissed off if I came back to the party soaking wet — which makes it all the more tempting. Suddenly, out of nowhere, there's a hand on my shoulder and a voice whispering in my ear.

"Thinking of another swim? Can I join you this time?"

I spin around to see who it is.

Costa.

I can tell by his sluggish words and the smell of ouzo on his breath that he's been drinking. Plus the fact that he's wavering back and forth, like he can barely hold himself up. *Ugh, this guy's so full of ick and ew.* Even though he's right about the swim, the last thing I want is to encourage him by admitting it. I shake my head and take a step backward. "No, thanks. I better get back to the party."

Whirling around, I head back to the restaurant. Too bad Costa's faster than me. He blocks my way and reaches for my hand. "What's your hurry? The water is perfect this time of night."

I freeze while Thalia's warning rings through my head. *Watch out for Costa — he has big eyes for beautiful girls.* I scowl and try to yank my hand back. "No, thanks. I said I'm not interested in a swim."

But he won't let go. Instead, he puts his other hand on my shoulder. Then he leans over me and grins. "Come on, *trela mou*. All I want is one kiss."

What? I try to slap him away, but he doesn't budge. "How dare you? I'm not your 'trailer moo'! Don't touch me!"

He laughs a snorty, sloppy laugh. Now his hands are on my waist, pulling me towards him. My dinner rises up in my throat. I push on his shoulders, trying to get away. But he's stronger than me. His arms encircle mine. *What's he doing?* Panicking, I try to raise my knee up to defend myself, but he's hugging me too tightly. His face burrows into my hair. I can hear his warm, panting breath in my ear.

"*Trela mou* — it means that you drive me crazy with love. And you smell so nice. Like a bouquet of summer flowers."

I try my best to scream, but the effort of trying to push him away is stealing all my breath. "Get away from me, you big dumb jerk!" I finally manage to grunt.

As I feel his hold tighten, I cast my eyes around the darkened beach, desperate to find someone who can help. Did anybody see me leave the party? Where's Mrs. Papadakis now that I finally need her? Then I see Thalia and her white lace dress emerging out of the darkness like a glowing ghost. She's walking towards me across the sand, but her head is turned to the ocean. She doesn't see me. I shout to get her attention. Before I know if she heard me or not, I hear someone else yelling and Nick is suddenly at my side, grabbing Costa's shoulder and pulling him off me.

"Leave her alone!"

Even though he's younger than Costa, Nick doesn't look afraid at all. He walks right up to him with his chest all puffed out like a rooster ready to fight and shoves him again on the shoulder. But Costa isn't afraid either. With his jaw clenched in anger, he pulls his good hand back to hit Nick. I react on pure instinct. Two years of Saturday morning karate instruction comes back to me in a rush and, without hesitation, I step forward, raise my knee, and square him hard in the groin with a triumphant, "Kiai!" Costa's eyes squeeze shut and his mouth drops open as if to scream, but the only sound that comes out of him is a tiny airless squeak. He lurches forward on Frankenstein feet, and I have to jump out of the way so he doesn't stumble into me. Finally, with a strangled moan, he drops to his knees in the sand. That's when Thalia sprints up. Her face is wide with panic.

"Oh my God! What's going on here?"

Her eyes flick from my upset face to Nick's angry one to Costa's guilty, pain-wracked expression. A look of understanding passes over her features. Fists punching her hips, she turns towards Costa and yells, "Again? How many times do we have to tell you to leave the guests alone? If my mother finds out, you'll be out of a job so fast your head will spin. Go to your room and sober up. I'll figure out what do with you tomorrow."

Still moaning, Costa holds up his hands in surrender. His dark eyes reach for mine. "You'll be sorry," I hear him growl under his breath. Then, without another word, he staggers away across the thick sand into the darkness. I let out a long, shuddery breath as I watch him go. My heart is still racing. Nick puts a gentle hand on my shoulder, his green eyes searching mine.

"Are you okay?"

I'm not okay. Not by a long shot. My head's spinning, my throat's closing up, and I can feel the prickly sting of tears pooling behind my eyes. But I don't want to let those tears out in front of Nick. I'll admit it, I turn really ugly when I cry. So I try never to cry in front of anyone, ever. Most especially not in front of a boy I like.

"Yeah, I'm okay," I say with a small nod, biting my bottom lip hard and struggling to hold the tears back.

"You sure?"

When I nod again, he turns and starts to run away in the same direction as Costa. "I'll be right back," he calls over his shoulder as he disappears into the darkness. "I want to follow him and make sure he's really heading home."

Suddenly exhausted, I sink down onto the sand.

"I just *knew* that crow was bringing bad luck," Thalia says, as Nick runs off into the night. I don't know how to reply to that. To me, those superstitions are just plain ridiculous. And anyway, I have more important things on my mind than birds and omens. A feeling of anger is growing inside me as my mind replays what just went down.

"You were totally right about that guy, Thalia. What a sleaze-ball. Do you think Sophia will fire him?"

With a loud sigh, she shakes her head and plops down beside me. "No, probably not."

I stare at her in shock. "But he attacked me! Nick was a witness. Why would she let him stay?"

She picks up a handful of sand and lets it fall slowly between her fingers.

"You know that story Costa told about his father the poor fisherman? Well, that poor fisherman is my father's brother."

I hear myself gasp as I connect the mental dots. "Costa's your cousin?"

She nods and reaches for another handful of sand. "After the accident, my uncle was scared that Costa would never work again because of his injury. The hotel was doing well, so my parents made a promise to take care of him. They brought him to work and live here at the hotel during the summers. He's been a waiter here ever since. He's a hard worker and never complains — but girls have always been a problem."

"But how can you let him stay on if he's attacking your guests?"

"It's only happened a couple of times. And it's always when he's overdone it on the ouzo. I mean, he's not really dangerous."

"How can you be so sure?"

"I've known him my whole life. He just thinks he's Casanova or something. He would have let you go after a kiss."

Somehow that's not very comforting. I stand up and start slapping the sand from the backs of my legs. "Well, thanks for warning me about him."

Thalia stands up too. "You're welcome. But if you don't mind, I'd like to give you another warning."

Her voice is suddenly a whisper, barely audible over the softly breaking waves behind us. I stop slapping my legs so I can hear better. "Sure."

She scratches her head and frowns, like she's searching for the right words. "Did Kat mention anything about …"

But her whisper melts into silence when Nick reappears from out of the darkness. "I followed Costa back to his room," he says, panting to catch his breath. "He won't give us any more trouble tonight. He's passed out in his bed." Then he reaches for my hand. "Do you want to go back to the party?"

As happy as I am to see him again, what I really want is to hear the rest of the warning. I smile and hold up a finger.

"I'd love to, in just one second." I tap Thalia's shoulder to let her know I'm still listening. "What were you saying? Did Kat mention anything about *what*?"

She pauses, almost like she's trying to collect her thoughts. Her eyes jump from my face over to Nick's, then back to mine. "It's nothing," she finally says with a shrug. "I … I just wanted to say that you're a very beautiful girl. And beauty attracts a lot of attention — both good and bad. Just be careful."

"Don't worry about Dani," Nick says, giving my hand a light squeeze. "I'll keep her safe."

Although he's speaking to Thalia, his eyes are glued to mine. Probably not the right moment to remind him that it was actually *me* who knocked Costa off his feet. With our hands linked together, he walks me back to the café, where the party is still going strong. I look for Kat but don't see her. She must have gone back to the room. Mrs. P is still dancing to the music, hopping in circles like a giant pigeon in her billowy grey dress. Nick guides me to a bench overlooking the dance floor. He holds tight to my hand. His fingers meld perfectly with mine. Like gears in a Swiss clock.

He doesn't leave my side for the rest of the night.

This is where the trip really starts to get interesting.

Chapter 7

• • • • • •

Dear Mom, you'll be happy to hear I've been learning a lot about the local culture. Last night I got a lesson in authentic Greek dancing and plate smashing ...

After Thalia's party, Nick and I become inseparable. Even though we haven't *officially* become a couple, he sits with me and Kat for all our meals and hangs out with us all day at the beach, talking and swimming and comparing music on our iPods. It's totally like we're together, except for one very important detail — I'm still waiting for him to kiss me. Every day after breakfast, we spread our towels out beside each other and lotion each other's backs to get ready for a long day in the sun. After a week, it's like we've known each other forever. I think there must be magic in meeting someone while you're on vacation, because every day feels like a month in real-life time. I know all the weird, random things about him that only a girlfriend would know. Like how the most ticklish part of his body is a hidden spot at the back of his left knee; how he was convinced he was related to Aquaman when he was little because two of his toes are webbed together; how his earlobes turn red when he's been in the sun too long; how he likes to dip his French fries in mayonnaise; how the only thing in the world he's really and truly afraid of is heights; how a guitar is the one thing he would bring if he got stranded on a desert island; and how his iPod is filled with really obscure old music from the '70s and '80s like Chilliwack and Styx. At the end of every day, I write all the details down in my travel journal. He's definitely something special. I don't want to forget anything.

The only problem? I'm getting more than a bit impatient. I never imagined I'd have to be the one to make the first move. But after a whole week has passed, it's beginning to feel like my only option. I know he's shy and all, but this is getting ridiculous. Why doesn't he want to kiss me? Every boy wants to kiss me. Don't think I'm bragging. It's the truth. Ever since fifth grade, they've been falling over themselves to be near me. Even creepy old Costa tried to kiss me. So is there some reason Nick's holding back? Am I losing my touch? Eating too much garlicky food? Is it possible he's gay?

One night, we're all enjoying a late dinner at the waterside café when Nick finally makes his move. Halfway through the meal, Kat excuses herself to use the washroom. As soon as we're alone, he nudges me with his foot under the table, takes a long breath, and says, "Hey, let's go on a date tonight."

Hallelujah! I put my fork down, flip my hair, and turn to look at him. "What are you talking about?" I ask coyly. A light blush begins to spread across his face.

"Well, I know we spend all day together but, uh ... we haven't had a real date yet. You know, just you and me going somewhere together. So what do you think? Do you want to do it tonight?"

Just at that moment, Costa walks up to the table balancing a large platter of grilled calamari on the palm of his good hand. When he sees Nick and me talking, he stops in his tracks with his dark eyes fixed on me. One of his bushy eyebrows is raised up in a perfect arc, while the other one is squished down over his eye. He kind of looks like a teenage pirate — except without the parrot or the gold teeth. With a scowl, he places the platter down at the opposite end of the table and marches back to the kitchen. I sigh with relief to see him go. I don't care if he *is* their nephew, how can Sophia and John let this guy keep working here?

"Dani? Did you hear me?"

Pushing Costa out of my thoughts, I turn back to Nick and smile as the platter of seafood makes its way around the table. "Yeah, okay. Where do you want to go?"

"I know a great place not far from here. It'll be perfect."

A night out without a chaperone? My heart bounces in my chest just thinking about it. I glance across the table and see Mrs. P staring at me with a forkful of calamari frozen in mid-air. Her lemon-sucking lips are working overtime and her eyebrows are arched halfway up her forehead. It's almost like she knows I'm up to something she won't approve of. Suddenly I feel guilty — although I'm not exactly sure why. Cupping a hand around my mouth, I lower my voice down to a barely audible whisper.

"But what about, you know … Mrs. P?"

Nick grins. "Sorry, she's not invited."

I poke him with my elbow. "Be serious."

He leans his face close to mine. "Don't worry. We'll sneak out after she's asleep."

His voice in my ear sends a trail of tingles up my neck. I shiver and nod eagerly. Really, how can I refuse?

It's around midnight when I sneak out of bed and inch into my clothes, so scared that the tiniest sound might rouse Mrs. P and put the kibosh on my big date. Holding my breath, I tiptoe out of our room and pull the door shut behind me without making even a whisper of a noise. Then I go to meet Nick on the front porch of the hotel. He's carrying a flashlight and there's a small knapsack slung over his back. All my anxiety disappears when he reaches for my hand.

"Ready?"

My stomach swirls with excitement. "Yeah, but where are we going?"

He grins mysteriously. "You'll see …"

We hike up the road for about a mile, holding hands the whole time. I'm grateful he thought to bring the flashlight because the road isn't lit at all. The further we stray away from the lights of the hotel, the blacker the night becomes. When the road ends, we walk for a few minutes across a dusty dirt path until we reach a dense grove of olive trees. Here, the moon and stars disappear and the night turns even blacker.

"It's just a bit further," Nick says, leading me into the grove.

Completely dependent on the flashlight now, we carefully make our way through the trees. Fallen twigs scratch at my feet and ankles as we stumble along in the dark. I'm wearing my flimsy leather beach sandals — not exactly the best shoes for a long hike. A thin branch snaps under my foot just as a cool breeze blows over my neck and shoulders. I shudder as my thoughts careen back to that night Costa attacked me on the beach. For a second, I can almost feel his thick licorice-scented breath panting in my ear. Suddenly, my heart seizes up with panic. *What are we doing out here in the middle of nowhere? How well do I know Nick anyway? Maybe this midnight date thing wasn't such a good idea after all.* A small part of me wants to run back to the hotel ... back to the safety of Mrs. P's watchful eye. Problem is, I can't turn back even if I want to. I need Nick and his flashlight. Another breath of wind blows over my neck, sending chills up my spine. Trying to keep calm, I reach out and touch his arm.

"How much further —"

Before I can finish my sentence, the trees give way and we're standing in front of a huge pile of massive marble blocks. I stop in my tracks and look around. The blocks are so stark white, they're practically glowing in the dark. I tug on Nick's hand. "What is this place?"

"Ancient ruins. Aren't they awesome? This island is littered with sites like this. Sophia told me that these are the remains of a temple dedicated to Demeter — the goddess of bread and nourishment."

We walk over to the massive blocks. Whatever doubts I had seem to have stayed behind in the olive grove. When we reach the nearest one, I reach out a hand and run my fingers over its pebbly surface. There are dozens of these giant rocks lying scattered across the ground — some piled on top of each other like a colossal version of a child's building block tower. Each one is about five feet high and six feet across. In a flash, Nick's scrambling up the side of the one I'm touching. When he gets to the top, he offers a hand down to help me up. I hesitate. "Are we allowed to do this?"

He smiles reassuringly. "I don't see any signs saying not to, do you? Just don't hurt anything."

Don't hurt anything? These blocks are ten times my size!

"There aren't any security cameras around here, are there?"

Nick lets out a laugh and waggles his hand to hurry me along. "Quit stalling and get up here, Dani. I'm supposed to be the one who's afraid of heights, remember?"

"Okay, okay." Pushing my nerves aside, I let him haul me up beside him. Once we're both on top, he slides the backpack off his shoulders, unzips the pocket, and pulls something out. My eyebrows shoot up in surprise.

"Food?"

Nick grins. "Yeah, I raided the kitchen so we could have a little snack in honour of good old Demeter. This is *baklava* — classic Greek dessert." He hands me a piece and takes one for himself. I pop it into my mouth. It's crispy and syrupy all at the same time. One bite and the sweet dough crumbles on my tongue.

Nick finishes his piece and offers me another. And then another. For the next few minutes, the sound of crunching pastry fills the moonlit ruins of Demeter's temple.

As soon as we're done eating all the dessert, he takes his backpack and arranges it at the head of the block.

"Your pillow, Karate Kid."

I giggle and lie down on the bumpy marble block. "Thanks, Aquaman." A small pang of guilt pokes at my conscience.

Why was I nervous? Nick is nothing like Costa.

I lean my head on the backpack and close my eyes. I feel totally safe with Nick. How could I have doubted him for even a second? "This is nice," I say as he stretches out beside me and the two of us stare up into the sky. A gasp flies from my lips when I see the stars. Why haven't I noticed them before? There seem to be thousands more of them than I've ever seen back home. And they're so much brighter. And they twinkle like diamonds — just like in that old nursery rhyme. I don't know why, but Toronto stars never twinkle like this. Beside me, I hear Nick sigh.

"I love looking at the sky when I'm on the islands. Away from city lights, you can see the constellations so clearly."

Constellations? I nod like I agree with him. But like math, astronomy's never made much sense to me. To my eyes, the night sky always looks like a confused jumble of tiny white dots.

Nick extends his right arm out and points upwards. "See that giant W? That's the constellation of Cassiopeia — she was a queen who was doomed to hang upside down in the sky because she was too vain and proud during her life on earth."

My eyes follow the direction of his finger. I have to squint a bit to make out the outline of the W.

"Hey, I see it!" I can't hide the excitement in my voice. Except for the Big Dipper, it's the first shape I've ever been able to make out in the stars.

Then Nick moves his finger down to the left. "Great, now look over there — that's Orion. He was raised up to the stars because he was the bravest hunter of all time. Can you see the three stars in his belt and his sword hanging down from it? And over there is Hercules, the great Greek warrior — he was like the Superman of the ancient world. Now look just south of Hercules. Do you see a group of stars that looks like a teapot? That's Asclepius — the god of medicine. He could bring people back from the dead."

"Really?"

"Yeah, the other gods put Asclepius up in the sky to honour his healing powers."

I shake my head in amazement. "That's incredible. How do you know all of this?"

He shrugs, and I feel his shoulders brush against mine. My heart knocks against my ribs. *Oh no, can he hear that?* "I'm Greek," he replies simply. "I grew up learning about these stories — they're part of our history. Just like these old ruins."

I nod and run my hands over the bumpy surface of the stone beneath me. I've never seen or touched anything so old before. I try to imagine all the people who've sat on these rocks over the thousands of years they've been lying here. My head fills with drawings of toga-wearing, olive-branch-wreathed ancient Greeks from our Grade 8 history book. Did teenagers from those days ever sneak out in the middle of the night to come stargaze in this spot? Or are we the first? I roll my head to the side so I can sneak a peek at Nick's profile. He's already staring at me with those incredible green eyes. I feel like there's a ping pong ball bouncing around in my stomach. He leans his face towards mine. I close my eyes and let out the breath I didn't know I'd been holding. Our lips meet softly. *Holy moly.* He's a good kisser. I put my hands on his shoulders and pull him a bit closer, breathing in the delicious mixture of smells that's spilling from his skin: coconut sunscreen, sea salt, and sweet baklava. It's perfect. Just like I knew it would be when I first saw him walk towards me in his bathing suit. Even though I'm lying on a hard slab of marble, I feel like I'm float-ing on air — stretched out atop the gates of heaven. All those constellations are swirling overhead like one of those paintings by that crazy old artist who cut off his ear for love.

A noise from behind startles me out of our kiss. I sit up and look around, half expecting to see Mrs. P watching us with a gloating "caught you" look on her face. But it's just another one of those stray cats. This one's white with orange spots. It's purring loudly as it curls up beside us on the ruins.

By the time we make it back to the hotel, it's past two o'clock in the morning. Feeling like a criminal, I tiptoe up to the door and turn the key as slowly and carefully as possible, trying to muffle the clicking sound of the lock. I can't even imagine what kind of trouble I'll catch if Mrs. P wakes up. Will she go ballistic? Try to ground me? Or worse, put me on a plane and send me back home early? You know what? Whatever happens, tonight's date with Nick was totally worth it.

Holding my breath, I slide the key back out of the lock, nudge the door open, and step into the room. What I see there makes my heart freeze.

Ohmygodohmygodohmygodohmygod …

Mrs. P is lying in her bed, facing the door, eyes wide open and staring right at me. A small scream rises in my throat, but I'm too petrified to let it out. Instead, I clench my teeth, close my eyes, and try to prepare myself for the inevitable explosion. I can hear my pulse pounding in my ears as I stand there in the dark. A full minute passes, but nothing happens. When I open my eyes and look again, I let out a shuddery sigh of relief. Maybe the late hour made my vision blurry, or maybe the shadows of the darkened room were playing tricks on me. But Mrs. P's eyes are closed and she's fast asleep. My racing heart slowly inches back to its normal pace.

I'm safe.

Without wasting another second, I pull on my pyjamas and creep into my bed as quietly as humanly possible. I stay up for a long time thinking about Nick. I can't wait to tell Kat all about what just happened. Tonight's date was everything I'd hoped for. It was perfect.

So perfect, in fact, that I completely forgot to ask Nick why he waited so long to ask me out.

Chapter 8

· · · · · ·

The next morning I invite Kat to go for a long walk so I can tell her all about my date with Nick. Costa's standing outside the waterside café, smoking and leering at us as we leave the resort. He's giving me that funny pirate look again as he puffs on a smelly cigarette. Ick! How could I ever have thought he was cute? His eyes connect with mine, sending a curl of nausea rolling through my stomach. My thoughts immediately fly back to that night on the beach. I shudder, remembering the feel of his hands on my waist, his face in my hair. *God, I hope he's not planning another one of his slimy Casanova moves.*

Just in case he is, I grab Kat's arm and hurry off in the other direction. We head away from the resort and far down the beach where it's safe to speak without anyone overhearing us. The last thing I want is for Nick to know I'm talking about him. Normally I wouldn't kiss and tell — but last night was so great, I just have to share the details with somebody. I figure Kat will appreciate hearing about it. She lives for those Harlequin novels, after all. And here's a real-life romantic adventure happening to me.

I talk for about twenty minutes, doing my best to remember every detail for her. The hike through the olive grove, the glowing ruins, the dessert, the stars … and, of course, the kiss. For some reason, Kat's unusually quiet after I finish. She definitely isn't gushing and swooning like I thought she would be. In fact, she isn't really saying anything at all. Slowing my steps, I turn and look at her. Her head is hanging low and her face is completely masked by a wavy curtain of hair.

"Kat? What's wrong?"

I lean over and try to read her expression. She's staring at her feet. That's when the world around us goes dark. I turn and look at the sky. There's a thick bank of clouds covering up the sun. Didn't Mrs. P say they didn't come out 'til winter? I shiver at the sudden loss of warmth.

"I — I can't believe you snuck out last night and didn't tell me," comes a small voice from behind the hair. *Uh-oh.* An awful itchiness begins to work its way across my skin. Kat's feelings are hurt. I don't need to see her face to get that. I squirm in my flip-flops, feeling guilty for leaving her out of the secret.

"Hey, I'm sorry I didn't tell you. But I … I just didn't want you to have to lie if your mother caught me. What if she found out you knew I was sneaking around with Nick? Then we *both* would have been in trouble."

She doesn't reply to that. Three slow waves roll in and out while I wait for her to say something. *Come on, Kat … look up …*

smile ... tell me it's okay. But she doesn't do any of those things. Instead, she just shuffles her toes with her face towards the sand like she's looking for buried treasure or something. My brain scrambles for a way to make this better. It takes me a while, but by the time the fourth wave rolls up the beach, a thought crosses my mind. An awful, cringe-inducing thought.

Oh no. Maybe it's bothering her that I have a boyfriend and she doesn't.

I open my mouth, ready to tell her that she doesn't have to worry, that I haven't forgotten about her, and that I'm still going to help her find a cute boy to kiss. But that's when something strange catches my eye. A funny-looking little girl with big blue eyes is walking towards us. She doesn't look more than eight or nine years old. She's dressed in rags, her hair is matted and knotted, and her skin is a deep brown — but I can tell from the way it's clumped around her knees and fingers that it's been darkened from dirt, not the sun. Although she's headed in the direction of the hotel, I can guess from her grungy appearance that she isn't a guest. She looks like something the ocean might have chewed up and spit out — so out of place on this pristine beach that I can't take my eyes off of her.

When she's about three feet away, she notices me staring at her. Raising a dirty finger into the air, she stops dead in her tracks and stares right back. My eyes lock with hers. I don't know how long she holds me there, imprisoned by that intense gaze. A coating of tiny pinpricks crawls over my skin. I want to move, but my feet feel frozen — like I'm standing in wet cement instead of sand. Her eyes are like water: cold, wet, bottomless. And floating on their surface is my own reflection, staring back at me.

Finally, Kat takes my wrist and gives it a shake. "Dani? You okay?"

Thank goodness for Kat, because at the sound of her voice the girl finally breaks her gaze and starts walking again. But I hear her mumbling something in a foreign language as she passes us. It takes a few seconds for my heart to stop racing and my voice to come back.

"W-why do you think she looked at me like that?" My words are quivering as they come out of my mouth. I take a deep breath, trying to calm myself down.

Stop being a drama queen, Dani. She's just a strange little kid, I tell myself.

But I'm not very convincing.

"I don't know," Kat replies, letting go of my wrist. "Maybe she's not used to seeing tourists on this part of the beach."

I rub at my arms, trying to erase the prickly sensation that's still lingering on my skin. "And what was that she said before she left?"

Kat shrugs. "I'm not sure. It didn't sound like Greek to me." She peers at me closely, like a doctor examining a feverish patient. "You okay? You look kind of pale. Do you want to turn back?"

I shake my head. My eyes follow the girl's trail of footsteps down the beach. She's walking in the direction of our hotel.

Another shiver passes over me at the thought of seeing her again. What I really want is to put as much space as possible between us.

"No, let's keep going for a bit."

Kat doesn't mention Nick again, so neither do I. But the guilt is still nibbling on my conscience. I promise myself not to sneak out without telling her again. And to get her that first kiss by the end of the summer. That'll put a smile on her face, I know it. You know it too, right?

After a few minutes, the sun comes back out from behind those dark clouds. We splash around in the shallow waves for a while before heading back to the resort. I try my best to forget about what happened there on the beach. But for some reason I just can't. All day long, the image of that strange, raggedy girl keeps coming back to haunt me. And later that night, she visits my sleep and peers into my dreams with her blue, staring eyes.

Chapter 9

Thalia was so wrong. The fish at the hotel isn't fresh after all. Two hours after eating what I thought was a perfectly good snapper from the restaurant's fish locker, I came down with a hideous case of food poisoning. I'll spare you the gory details, but let's just say it wasn't a pretty scene in the bathroom that night. Or the next day either. And in between all the waves of puking, I felt so sick that all I could do was lie in bed and wait for the nausea to go away. Kat felt sorry for me, but I could tell by her wrinkled-up nose that she didn't want to hang around the barf chamber any longer than she had to.

"You don't mind if I go to the beach while you're resting, do you?" she asks the next morning. "My mom is here to take care of you."

I shake my head and wave her off. She grabs her swimsuit and bolts for the door. For the first time since we left Toronto, I actually don't mind hanging out with Mrs. P. The instant I got sick she sort of transformed into my own personal angel of mercy. She stayed with me the whole time, holding my hair back whenever I spewed chunks and cleaning out my vomit bucket when I got too weak to make it to the toilet. She stayed at my bedside for hours on end and held my glass of ginger ale while I took tiny sips through a straw. For the first time in my life, I'm beginning to appreciate this old-school mom thing. I mean, geez, my own mother never even made such a fuss over me before. If I wasn't feeling so disgusting, I'd actually enjoy all the attention. But my flip-flopping stomach is making it impossible to enjoy anything.

Time passes in a fuzzy green blur. "Why am I the only one who got sick from that fish?" I whine, sometime during day two of my puke party. Is it morning? Afternoon? My head's too woozy to figure it out.

"You're probably just not as accustomed to the Greek food as the rest of us," Mrs. P replies, wiping my sweaty face with a cool cloth. I groan and roll over onto my side to fight off a fresh onslaught of cramps. I think about my friends enjoying the beach and swimming in that silvery blue ocean and feel even sicker.

"I miss Nick," I moan into my pillow.

Mrs. P takes my hand. "Of course you do, Daniella. And I'm sure he misses you too. You know, he told Katerina that he wants to come visit and see if you're all right. But I said no. I'm sure you don't want him to see you in this, um … unfortunate condition, do you?"

I shake my head. She's right. I haven't showered yet. I'm sure I reek of vomit, and my skin's probably a gross shade of green.

Mrs. P tilts her head towards me and stares at me with those dark eyes of hers. There's a gleam in there that I've never seen before. Is it kindness? Can it be possible that this woman is actually beginning to like me?

"Nicholas is a wonderful boy — handsome, kind, respectful. I've known him since the day he was born." She raises her eyebrows and smiles. "Have I noticed that you two seem to be getting especially close lately?"

I nod and think back to the night at the ruined temple. Closing my eyes, I try to remember the feeling of kissing him under that canopy of stars. "I ... I think I might be falling in love with him," I whisper.

I don't know if Mrs. P heard me or not, because when I open my eyes again she's in the bathroom refreshing my cool cloth. When she comes back she sits down beside me on the bed and places it gently on my forehead.

"Being back in Greece always reminds me of my childhood," she says, stroking my hair tenderly away from my face. "My family wasn't wealthy, but we were very happy. I moved to Toronto right after I was married, but I left my heart here on the islands. Even though I've lived in Canada for more than half of my life, I will always be Greek first. When tradition and culture grow inside you, it's very hard to change your ways — no matter where you go in life. Now that you've seen it here, I'm sure you understand. When the Greek ways get into your blood, they never let go."

She pauses here and her eyes go slightly out of focus — like she's seeing something that isn't really there. "Raising my daughter in Canada hasn't been easy," she continues, her voice rising with emotion. "As hard as I've tried to teach her the 'old ways,' I often wonder if she really understands what it means to be Greek. Sometimes I worry that no matter what I do, modern ways will win over tradition. And that my Katerina will grow up to be Canadian first ... not Greek."

I have no idea why Mrs. P is telling me this stuff. But in a weird way, I kind of don't mind. The sound of her voice is soothing — sort of like a lullaby. She's still talking about tradition when I feel my eyes close and my body begin to fall into a deep sleep.

Strange dreams fill my head. First, I dream about the strange girl with the blue eyes. She's here in the hotel room with me, sitting by my bed as I twist and turn under the sheets. And when I ask for her help getting up, she puts a dirty hand to her face, pulls out her left eyeball, and drops it on my pillow.

Then I dream Costa is running after me, catching me from behind and pulling me with him into the ocean. The feel of his stinking, wet breath on my neck is so real, my body freezes with panic. I scream a silent dream-scream and then he disappears like a ninja.

Next, I dream I'm back home with my family in Toronto. My parents are gushing over me and telling me how much they love me and my older sisters are actually being nice to me for a change. They even hug me. Which is how I know it's not real. My sisters have bought me presents — new purses and clothes and jewellery. And they drape them over my arms and neck like I'm a doll they're playing dress-up with. And I'm loving every moment of it.

Finally, I dream about Kat. We're back at school together and it's Grade 9 now. She's walking down the hall like she owns the place — bold steps and bright eyes, wearing confidence like other kids wear hoodies. The sadness is gone from her eyes. And even though it's just a dream, somehow I know it's gone for good.

Maybe that last dream is what finally cures my stomach, because when I wake up the next morning, I don't feel like puking anymore. I sit up in bed and smile because, for the first time in two days, my insides aren't turning cartwheels. I feel like myself again.

"What time is it? Where's Kat?" I ask, easing myself out of bed.

Mrs. P hurries to my side and holds my arm until she's sure I'm steady on my feet. "It's almost noon. Katerina and Nicholas left for the beach about an hour ago."

"Great. I'll go and meet them there." I shuffle over to the dresser and pull out my bathing suit.

"Oh no. You're not ready to go out yet, *cardio mou*," Mrs. P clucks. "You need at least another day of rest to get your strength back."

But I've already wasted enough of my trip in bed. There are only three days left before we have to go home to Toronto and I want to soak up every remaining minute of the beach and the water. And Nick.

"Don't worry, I'm fine," I insist, heading to the bathroom to clean up and get dressed. Once I'm showered and wearing my swimsuit, I check myself out in the mirror. Ugh. My body looks scary skinny from all that yacking. I'll have to eat tons of that yummy Greek fried cheese tonight to start gaining some of my curves back. Just the thought of it brings pools of water to my mouth. Yup, my appetite is definitely restored. I reach for my brush and give my hair a hundred strokes.

When I finally emerge from the bathroom, Mrs. P hands me my leather sandals and a fully packed beach bag. "There's a snack in there in case you get hungry," she says.

Man, a girl could really get used to this kind of service. "Thanks," I say, taking my stuff from her.

The skin between her eyes is pinched tight like a raisin. "But I really think you're rushing things, Daniella," she adds. "Come right back if you feel sick at all."

"Yeah, yeah. I will," I say. But I don't really mean it. Nothing's keeping me off that beach now. Hoisting the bag up on my shoulder, I slip on my sandals then reach out to give her a hug. Her hair smells of honey and almonds — like a yummy Greek dessert. My mouth starts to water again at the thought of food.

"Thanks for taking such good care of me these past few days," I whisper into her ear. Mrs. P hugs me back. Her body feels surprisingly small and frail in my arms. I wonder how I could have misjudged this woman so badly? After she's been so kind to me, I almost feel bad leaving her behind in the lonely hotel room. But the ocean is calling my name.

"See you at dinner," I say, stepping away from her. With a wave, I hurry out the door before she can find another reason to call me back.

It feels kind of funny walking again. The muscles in my legs and feet are stiff from two days of lying in bed. But I'm so eager to see Nick, I force myself to hurry as I start down the slippery rock stairs.

Will Nick be as excited to see me as I am to see him? Will he sweep me up into his arms and twirl me around like he did to Kat back on that first day? Did Kat find someone to kiss while I've been away sick?

I can't wait to find out. But halfway down the stairs all my big plans for the beach shatter like glass when I feel something snap on my sandal. My left ankle twists under itself and a searing pain shoots up my leg. A scream of terror flies from my lips as I lose my balance and pitch forward. Craggy stones bite into my skin as I dive head over heels down the side of the rocky hill. I lie crumpled in a pathetic heap at the bottom. Tangled bones and broken spirit.

This doesn't look good, you whisper.

Smart cookie.

Chapter 10

• • • • • • •

They tell me I have to spend the rest of my vacation on crutches. Can you believe it? I know, right? Completely made of suck.

After fitting me with a tensor bandage and instructing me to stay off my foot, the doctor at the local hospital tries to make me feel better about the accident. "You should be happy it's only sprained," he says, clicking his pen in and out as he prepares to sign my release papers. "By the looks of those scrapes you sustained in the fall, this ankle could have been a lot worse. You're a lucky girl."

Lucky? Happy?

Please!

What do I have to be happy about? I can't go swimming or ride the scooters or hike over to the ruins for another date with Nick. I can't take that windsurfing lesson I had booked. Or the paddleboard yoga class either. It's a totally craptastic way to end my last days in Greece.

Dear Mom, wait 'til you hear what happened today. I got an inside tour of the emergency room of an authentic Greek medical facility. I miss home.

Nick and Kat are trying to help me feel better. They're running around opening doors for me and making sure I'm comfortable. And of course Mrs. P's happily put her "angel of mercy" cap back on. As much as I like all the attention, I'm still pretty bummed. I've never been hurt this badly in my life.

When we get back to the hotel room, Kat does her best to cheer me up. "Let's go to the beach. It's low tide — maybe we can build a sandcastle."

But I don't want to go. "No," I pout. "I don't want anyone seeing me looking this rough." It's the truth. After falling down that hill, I have enough scrapes and bruises to colour a rainbow. So instead, Kat does some funny impersonations to help my mood. She does the doctor with twitchy eye and clicky pen. She does big, lumbering Theo John. She even does a silly one of me hobbling around on my crutches with some exaggerated fake barfing.

It helps. A bit.

Okay, a lot.

Before long, she has me in stitches. The non-medical kind, of course. "How did you get so good at impersonations?" I giggle as she flops onto the bed beside me. "Did you take acting classes when you were young?" She shakes her head and stares up at the white bumps on the ceiling. I wait a long time for her to answer.

"I guess sometimes it's just easier to pretend to be someone else," she finally says. Her voice sounds small and hollow. I'm not sure what she means by that. But it can't be anything good because the sad look is floating back into her eyes now. I change the subject fast, before it settles in for a meal.

"I think I'm ready for the beach now." I stand up, careful not to put too much weight on my bad ankle. "Maybe we can catch the sunset."

She bounds off the bed and helps me hobble down the long paved road to the beach. She chats like she's all happy even though I can see from her eyes there's something dragging her heart down. Then when Nick joins us, she gets even quieter. I wish I was smart enough to understand why. The three of us build a sandcastle together. We work hard on it, but still it ends up looking more like a crumbling Greek ruin than a castle. I pull out my camera to take a photo, so my parents will think I'm taking an interest in local beach art. "Smile, Kat," I plead. "Don't make me come over there and tickle you."

The least she can do is perk up for the camera, right?

Wrong.

At least Nick looks happy in the photo. More than happy actually. In every picture I take of him, he looks like he can reach through the lens with his grin and his perfect white teeth. "You make me feel like that," he tells me later when we're alone after dinner, scrolling through the photos. "Like there's a carnival happening in my head, all day, every day."

I peer at him closely. "A good carnival or a crappy, broken-down one?"

"A good one. A great one. The kind where they sell cotton candy on a cone."

"Pink?"

He nods. "Blue too. Made in front of you in one of those round fluffy machines."

"Are there rides?"

He puts an arm around me. "Big, fast, spinny ones. And ponies. All free with admission. And no lines." He pins me to my seat with those golden-green eyes. "How do you do that to me, Dani?"

I shrug and smooth back my hair, all casual and easy. Like my heart isn't flipping like a Cirque du Soleil acrobat. "I don't know," I say, flashing him my signature smile.

That's not a lie, by the way. Just between us, sometimes I wonder why Nick likes me so much. And why Kat likes me too, for that matter. I know I'm pretty — people have been telling me that since I was old enough to talk. But I'm not the nicest girl around. And I'm definitely not the smartest. Sometimes I worry that my inside doesn't match up to my outside. I know my parents like me because they have to. And my sisters don't really seem to like me much at all. I tell myself there is good inside me. I know it's there. I can feel it. I think you could see it too if you were willing to look hard enough. I promise it's there. Just under the surface. Like one of those tiny, newborn freckles you get in the summer. You know the little ones that seem to float just under your skin? The ones you can only see it if you look close enough … if you focus your attention for long enough?

Kat wakes me up way too early the next morning. "There's something I want to talk to you about," she whispers, rocking my shoulder gently. I open my sleep-crusted eyes to see her leaning over my pillow. Her morning breath blows under my nose. It smells like the ocean.

"What?" I mumble.

"Not here. Let's go down to the beach."

I blink a couple of times to make sure this isn't a dream. "Right now? I'm tired," I say, muffling a yawn.

"This is important, Dani. It really can't wait." Her voice is so low, like it's crawling out of her stomach.

Okay. So I'm intrigued enough to drag myself out of bed. Kat's never been this mysterious before. Curiosity fuels my sloppy bones. When we get to the beach, we order some iced lattes from the café and find a good table in the sun. I let Kat take a couple of sips of her drink before I start digging for answers.

"I'm going crazy with suspense. What's so important?"

With a sigh, she puts a hand on my shoulder. She has this look on her face like she's about to announce something really awful. Like she ran over a puppy with her scooter. "I'm not sure how to say this," she starts, shaking her head.

Is that pity in her eyes? "Not sure how to say what?" I ask, forcing my lips into a smile. Like I don't have a care in the world. Like it's not totally irking me to be the object of pity.

"It's about all the bad luck you've been having."

Kat's hand is starting to feel uncomfortably heavy on my shoulder. I shift my chair to the left, but she just shifts along with me. "I know, right? It's like I'm cursed or something," I say.

She leans so close, I can see the tiny beads of sweat lining her upper lip. "Yes," she says. "That's exactly what I've been thinking too. I was trying to figure it out the whole time you were at the hospital. But it wasn't until we got back from the beach last night that I finally got it."

"Got what?" I demand. I wish she'd get to the point. The sun is hot this morning. I lift my hair off the back of neck where I'm starting to sweat. I try to wiggle her hand off my shoulder, but it isn't budging. "What are you talking about, Kat?"

"I think it's the —" She pauses and looks around to make sure no one's listening. Then her voice lowers to such a quiet whisper, I can barely make out the words. "— the Evil Eye."

"What are you talking about?" I pick up my napkin to shoo away a bee that's buzzing around our table. "What's the Evil Eye?"

I guess my question must surprise her because her mouth falls open and stays that way for so long, I can see all the fillings in her back molars. "Better be careful, Kat, or that bee is going to fly right in," I tease. Finally, after a good ten seconds, she picks her jaw back up and finds her voice again.

"Are you serious, Dani? You mean you've never heard of the Evil Eye before?"

I shrug and take a sip of my latte. "Nope."

Her grip on my shoulder tightens even more. Ouch! For such a skinny girl, she's surprisingly strong. "Listen to me," she says.

"The Evil Eye is a terrible curse. Everyone in Greece knows about it. Mummy says it gives you bad luck — like, *really* bad luck. You can get sick, lose all your possessions, even die. I mean, why do you think she makes me wear this?" She lifts her wrist so I can see her bracelet with all the funny blue eyeballs. "And she once told me that beautiful people are *especially* at risk of getting the Evil Eye, so I'm thinking that's what's happened to you."

I stare at Kat in shocked silence. Is she going crazy? This is a bit too voodoo for me. *Um, hello? We're Canadian. Pretty sure we don't have curses and bad luck spells in Canada.*

Using both hands, I peel her death grip off my shoulder. "You don't really believe that stuff, do you?" I finally reply. "Sorry, but it's just ... well, dumb."

Kat gasps. And then she leans over and spits. Just like her mother.

"Ptoo ... ptoo ... ptoo ..."

"Stop that!" I yelp, glancing around to see if anyone else is watching.

Wiping her mouth with the back of her hand, she straightens back up. Her eyes are glistening. "This is serious, Dani. I'm telling you, every Greek knows that the Evil Eye is powerful. Remember that day on the beach? I saw the way that little girl looked at you. She gave the Evil Eye to you for sure. I think you should ask my mother about this. She knows all about these old curses. I think we should talk to her and see if she can help you."

A chill runs up my back just at the thought of that strange girl and her cold, bottomless eyes. But if Kat's trying to scare me,

I'm not going to let it work. "No, thanks, I'll be fine. Really." I fold my arms across my chest and shake my head. The bee's still circling around and around our table, like it's waiting for clearance to land. "Anyway," I add, "I thought you said you weren't superstitious."

Her hand flies up in my face. She's in full defence mode now. "I'm not superstitious. I told you, it's just my mother."

"Okay, so just tell her thanks but no thanks. Now are we done? Because I want to go see if Nick's awake."

Kat's face is like a landslide. "Did you hear anything I just said? I'm telling you that you could be *cursed*. Which means that you're in a lot of danger — and if you hang out with Nick you'll be putting him in danger too. You have to talk to Mummy and see if she can cure you."

That's the point when I begin to feel very uncomfortable with the conversation. Earlier this year, my Grade 8 history teacher told our class that the Greeks were brilliant thinkers and philosophers and invented democracy and all kinds of other important stuff. At the time, I remember being pretty impressed that Kat came from such an intelligent gene pool. So how is it possible that such a civilized nation can be so crazed with superstitions? With an irritated sigh, I reach for my room key.

"I don't want to talk about this anymore. I mean, you *do* realize how totally ridiculous this sounds, right? Like, how can you possibly believe in this Evil Eye mumbo-jumbOW!"

Suddenly, the bee that's been buzzing around our table lands on my hand and jabs its stinger right into me. A sharp, burning pain erupts over my skin. I scream, drop my key, and jump up from my chair — forgetting, of course, all about my injured ankle. I scream even louder this time as searing knives of pain shoot up my leg. I sink back into my chair, squeeze my eyes shut, and will myself not to cry. Kat scoops an ice cube out of her latte, wraps it in a napkin, and presses it to my sore hand. The cold is a shock, but little by little it helps to kill the pain. When I open my eyes again, she's shaking her head sadly and tsking with her tongue. *More pity? Get me out of here!* She opens her mouth to speak, but my good hand flies up to stop her.

"Don't say it. Please?"

She shrugs and stays quiet. But it's too late. You and I both know exactly what she's thinking.

Chapter 11
· · · · · · ·

Dear Mom, I spent the last few days of my trip learning about awkward Greek superstitions. I would write more about them, but I'm not going to bother. You'd never believe me anyway ...

It's the morning of our flight back to Canada. We're all gathered on the hotel porch waiting for the taxi to take us to the airport. Sophia's crying as she kisses and hugs Mrs. P and Kat and Nick. But her tears flow even harder when she comes to me. "Please come back again soon," she says, wrapping me up in her soft arms. "By next summer, I'll have a real staircase built down to the beach so it will be safe."

Poor Sophia. I know how guilty she felt after my accident. Like it's somehow her fault that I took the unofficial shortcut. "It's okay," I say and smile to make her feel better. "It's my fault, anyway. I should have taken the long way down."

When it's John's turn, his hug is so forceful, it almost knocks me off my crutches. "You're always welcome here!" he says. Whoa.

Those must be the first words he's said to me all trip. His voice is so deep, I can feel the sound waves. A hard lump rises in my throat. As awful as the past week's been, I'm going to miss these guys.

Then Thalia kisses me goodbye — three times on the cheeks, as per the Greek custom.

Mwah.

"Don't forget what I told you that night on the beach," she whispers on my left cheek. My thoughts fly back to that night.

"Remind me what that was again?" I whisper back as she swoops in for my right cheek.

Mwah.

"Just promise me you'll be careful," she says on the final kiss.
Mwah.

Huh? Careful of what? Before I can ask her to explain, I hear the sound of tires scrunching up the gravel driveway behind me. Our taxi's here. Thalia takes a small step back. "Just be safe and keep your eyes open. All right?"

Is she talking about my ankle? "Don't worry. There aren't any slippery rock slopes in my neighbourhood back home."

She's supposed to laugh at my joke. But she doesn't even crack a smile.

Weird.

We arrive at the airport two hours before the flight and there's already a huge lineup of people at the Canada-Air counter. Nick tells some jokes while we wait for the line to slowly inch forward, but Kat isn't laughing at any of them. She's been acting so weird around Nick lately ... like she's annoyed with him or something.

I have a nagging feeling it has to do with the fact that he's spending so much time with me. I make a mental note to ask her about it when we get back to Toronto. Leaning on her suitcase, Mrs. P watches us and sucks lemons. At least some things never change. When it's finally my turn to check in, I hobble up to the counter and give the agent my ticket. "Could I get a window seat please?" I ask, smiling my sweetest smile.

"I'll see what I can do. Your passport, please?"

I reach into the pouch where I keep all my important travel stuff, but don't see it. I flip through all the compartments and flaps and slots but my passport isn't there. My stomach does a weak somersault.

"Just a second," I say, bending down to look through my carry-on bag. A tight knot of fear begins to form inside my chest. When's the last time I saw my passport, anyway? I can't remember. I look in every pocket and every flap of my bag. I double and triple check my travel pouch. But it still isn't there.

It isn't anywhere.

My eyes grow so wide with nerves, it feels like they might pop out of my head. I look back at the ticket agent. Her name tag reads: "Elena."

"It's not here. I — I can't find it! But I promise I'm Canadian. Call my mom if you want." I smile my most convincing smile.

Elena doesn't even flinch.

"I'm sorry, but you cannot board the plane without the appropriate travel documents. Please step aside."

Oh my God. With the knot of fear growing bigger by the

second, I limp out of the line and lay my bags out on the floor to search them. Nick and Kat help me look while Mrs. P dials up Sophia on Kat's cellphone and asks her to search the hotel room. I can feel my whole body break out into a nervous sweat as I empty out my carry-on and then my suitcase. I look everywhere, but no passport. I feel like I'm losing my mind. Where could it have gone? Nick rubs my shoulders, trying to comfort me.

"Don't worry, we'll help you find it. It must be around here somewhere."

After yet another check of the suitcase, I hear Kat's cellphone go off. Mrs. P clicks it on and begins speaking in Greek. It has to be Sophia calling back. I hold my breath and wish for good news. *Please, please, please ...*

A second later, Mrs. P shakes her head as she snaps the phone shut.

"Sorry, Daniella. Sophia and John turned the room upside down. They didn't find your passport anywhere."

The news is like a boulder falling on my head. How am I going to get out of this country? Suddenly, I want to be home so badly it hurts. I want my parents, my room, my bed, even my awful sisters. This totally must be how Dorothy felt in *The Wizard of Oz*. My eyes fill up with tears, but I bite the inside of my cheek to keep them from falling. I'm not going to let myself cry in front of all these people. And especially not Nick.

"What am I going to do?" I ask, unable to stop my voice from shrinking into a whine. "Our flight's leaving in an hour. Are they going to let me go home?"

Mrs. P walks back to the counter and begins speaking to Elena the ticket agent again. A flurry of Greek flies back and forth between them while I try to hold back those persistent tears. I bite the inside of my other cheek so hard I can taste blood. Kat stands next to me and holds my hand. None of us move a muscle while we wait to see what Elena will say. Finally Mrs. P turns back to me and sighs.

"She says we must go speak to the Canadian Embassy. If we explain what happened, they can probably issue a temporary passport to get you home."

Temporary passport? A small spark of hope springs up inside my heart. "How long will that take? Will I still make my flight?"

She speaks softly, as if she's worried the truth might shatter me to pieces. "No, you won't make it onto this flight. But there's another one taking off for Toronto in ten hours. We'll probably be able to make that one. Don't worry, Daniella — I'll help you sort this all out and get you home."

Ten hours? My spark of hope disintegrates into crumbs. *No! I want to go home now!* But before I can utter a word of protest, Mrs. P turns to Nick and Kat and points back to Elena.

"There's no reason why you should have to wait around. You two go ahead and board the plane together. I'll call Mr. Papadakis and have him meet you in Toronto when you land. Once we have the passport figured out, I'll follow with Daniella on the next flight."

What?

Nick moves closer and reaches for my hand. His golden-green eyes are all squinty with worry. At any other moment, I probably would have thought it was adorable. But right now I'm just too upset to care about anybody but myself.

"Mrs. Papadakis, I don't want to go back to Canada without Dani," he says. "I'll stay here and help her get her passport."

Oh, Nick, I think I really do love you. For a split second, I actually start to feel better. It won't be so bad hanging around here if I can be with Nick. It might even be kind of fun being here all by ourselves. Nine hours alone in a foreign country with the cutest guy this side of Canada? Kind of sweet. I'm actually starting to get excited when Mrs. P shakes her head and squashes the plan to pieces.

"No. Katerina needs to get home immediately. She's teaching enriched Greek school in August and the first class starts tomorrow morning. I don't want her to miss it and I don't want her travelling alone."

Kat's face flashes a mortified shade of red. "It's okay, Mummy. I can miss one day."

Mrs. P plants her hands on her hips and shakes her head again. "Absolutely not. The children and parents will be expecting you there. You'll go home with Nicholas."

Man, this woman is tough as nails. She reminds me of the Greek warrior Nick told me about that night on the ruins. What was his name again? That's right. Hercules — the ancient Superman. I wouldn't be surprised to find out that the two of them are distantly related or something. I mean, Mrs. P could totally have warrior blood. But maybe Nick has some warrior blood, too. Because even though I'm ready to give up the fight right then and there, he stands his ground.

"If the Greek school is that important, why don't *you* go home with Kat, Mrs. Papadakis?" he says. "I can stay here with Dani and get the passport figured out."

Unfortunately, his suggestion brings Mrs. P to the end of her rope. Her eyes darken.

Better stand back.

"Listen to me, young man," she says, pointing her finger at Nick. "I made a promise to Mrs. Price that I would take care of this girl. I will not abandon her in a foreign country with a boy who can't even take care of a group of nine-year-old campers. Now stop arguing with me, Nicholas. This is the only way."

And that's that. With a heavy heart, I watch as Kat and Nick get their boarding passes and head for the security check. "I'm so sorry about all this, Dani. I wish I didn't have to go," Nick says as he gives me a little kiss goodbye. "Call me as soon as you get home. I'll be waiting."

All I can do is nod.

"Are you sure you'll be okay?" Kat asks, throwing her arms around me.

"Sure. No problem," I manage to squeak. I'm trying so hard to be brave in front of Nick. But really, it feels like there's an avalanche crushing my stomach. I've never felt sorry for myself before. It sucks.

Kat's still hugging me. "The Evil Eye is responsible for this," she whispers in my ear. "I told you bad things were going to keep happening. You need to get this cured fast, Dani." She finally releases me and I struggle to erase the "whatever" off my face.

"I'll see you back in Toronto," I say instead.

I wave as they walk up the stairs towards security. Nick turns to me and waves back but Kat's busy chatting about something and doesn't seem to notice. I'm too upset to breathe as I watch them disappear into the crowd. I want to be on that plane so badly. I want to be heading home with my friends, not lining up at a government office with my chaperone. It's not fair. Is this how jealousy feels? I've honestly never been jealous of anyone in my life until this moment.

Mrs. P helps me with my suitcase as I limp along with her back to the exit. "Don't worry, Daniella," she says, patting my shoulder. "I won't leave your side until this whole mess is all sorted out."

That makes me want to cry more than anything.

TORONTO

Chapter 12

• • • • • • •

Those twenty hours with Mrs. P were awful. You knew they would be, right? The lineup at the embassy was a mile long and she scolded me the whole time we were waiting in it.

You should take better care of your travel documents. You're lucky I'm here to help you. I know what your problem is: too much attention on boys, not enough attention on what's really important. When I was your age, I was practically running my family's entire household. You kids today are so careless. Why is responsibility such a foreign concept for you? Would you forget your head if it wasn't screwed on? Blah ... blah ... blah ...

Multiply that by a million and you'll begin to get an idea of what I had to deal with while waiting for my passport. It was positively soul-crushing. I honestly don't know how Kat puts up with it. Mrs. P's the kind of person who only sees what's wrong with a thing. Never what's right. I guess for some people, it's easier to see the bad stuff. Maybe because the bad floats to the top. Like an oil spill.

When we finally get to the front of the line, she spends five minutes rummaging through her purse for a pen, and I'm terrified those bat bones Kat warned me about are going to fall out and land on my feet. By the time we get my temporary travel papers, a stress headache is starting to push into my brain. It's so painful, it helps me forget about my twisted ankle for a while. When we finally get on the plane, it's eight o'clock at night and I'm exhausted. As we make our way to our seats, I think about what Kat said about the curse. *If there's anything to that Evil Eye thing, you guys are going down with me,* I think, looking at the rows of faces flying to Canada with us. It's nice to have something to laugh about after the heinous day I just had.

Mrs. P falls asleep almost immediately after the takeoff, which is a relief. But not for long because, apparently, sleeping in an upright position makes Mrs. P snore. And her snoring isn't o f the soft, purring kitty-cat variety. It's an air-sucking, throat-catching, mucus-snorting mess. I ask a passing flight attendant if I can change seats, but — just my luck — the plane's full and there's nowhere to go. At least he's sympathetic to my situation and gives me a flimsy pillow to cover my ears and muffle the sound. There are a couple of times when I find myself starting to drift off to sleep, but inevitably the snoring gets louder and wakes me up again. For a while there, I'm actually wishing for the plane to crash into the ocean and put me out of my misery. Yeah, it's *that* bad.

Finally I hobble to the smelly airplane bathroom with my pillow, curl up on top of the toilet lid, and catch a nap in there. But not long after, I'm jolted awake by the sound of a decidedly *un*sympathetic flight attendant pounding on the door.

"What's going on in there? There's no smoking on the plane!"

"No, I'm not smoking," I call out. "I'm just trying to get some sleep."

Another round of door pounding rattles the walls around me. "The captain has switched on the seat belt sign. You'll have to come out now!"

Needless to say, I've never been so happy to see my parents in my life. When they meet me at the airport, I hug them so long and hard, they have to pry me out of their arms. They drive me home in Rosie — my red Mini Cooper. They even surprise me with a new personalized licence plate for her. *DanizCar*. Cute, right?

Okay, I know what you're thinking. *What's a not-quite-four-teen-year-old doing with her own car?* It's actually the Dreadful Duo's old ride. But when my sisters each got new cars for university, Mom and Dad decided to keep Rosie for when I get my driver's licence in a couple of years. But that felt like way too long to wait, so I convinced Dad to let me practice a bit in the meantime. Now when he takes Rosie out once a week to keep her engine in good shape, he usually lets me have a quick turn at the wheel. You know, just empty parking lot kind of stuff. We've been doing it since the snow melted last April. Not to brag or anything, but I think I'm already a pretty good driver.

Okay, sure, it's *technically* against the law. But I'm not too worried about getting stopped by a cop. For one thing, I've got Dad with me. Plus I've talked and smiled my way out of lots of trouble before. There's no doubt in my mind that I could wiggle myself out of a traffic ticket if I had to.

When I walk back into my house, I think I actually might break down and start crying with relief. It feels so good to be home again, I even hug my dreadful sisters, Toby and Charley, who are both so shocked that they don't even push me away. It's almost like the surreal dream I had that night in Greece when I was sick.

While Dad brings my bags in from the car, I limp upstairs to my room, sink onto my bed, and hug my pillow and duvet like they're a pair of long-lost friends. Believe me, you never realize how much you'll miss the things that are important to you until there's a chance you'll never see them again.

I sigh deeply and flip onto my back as my eyes greedily gobble up the familiar details of my room. My lavender walls — the colour that I insisted on when I was ten because it was the biggest colour on the Paris runways that year. My walk-in closet, overflowing with my collection of clothes, shoes, and purses. Then there's my wall of photos of me and my friends — with a couple of blank places where I took down pictures of Alec the Hockey Jerk right before leaving for Greece. I make a mental note to put up a few of Nick once I get my vacation photos printed. I catch my reflection in one of the little jewelled mirrors that hang in a circle above my dresser. My tan looks fab, but my eyes are all tired and stressed. Hopefully it's nothing a good night's sleep won't fix. I want to be sure to look perfect for Nick when we see each other again.

"Knock-knock, Danz," Dad says, walking through the door with my bags. "Do you need any help unpacking?"

Dropping my pillow, I sit up and swing my legs off the bed. "No, thanks. I'll be okay."

"Come down when you're done. We want to hear all about your trip. Don't start getting on the phone with all your friends before we've had a chance to talk to you first."

I snort under my breath. *What friends?* All of them are still away at overnight camp. Right now, the only friend I have left in the city is Kat. And, of course, Nick.

Just the thought of him perks me up. Now that we're back in Toronto, I can't wait to see his house, meet his friends, introduce him to my parents. My cellphone starts ringing, breaking through my daydream. *Maybe it's him,* I think, scrambling around my room to answer it as fast as my crutches will allow. Kneeling down on my pink carpet, I follow the muffled sound of Daft Punk's "Get Lucky" as I burrow through my stuff. I check my purse, my jacket pocket, my carry-on bag — but no phone. Just when I think my voice mail is going to click on, I find it tucked inside one of my purple Chucks at the bottom of my suitcase. I pull it out and flip it open, trying to ignore the smelly-foot stink that's clinging to the plastic cover.

"Hello?" I breathe, smiling my signature smile. I don't know why — it's not as if Nick can see me through the phone.

"Hey, you're back! How was the flight? Did Mummy drive you crazy? She did, didn't she?"

"Kat? Slow down." She's talking so fast it's hard to make out her words.

"I'm so sorry I couldn't stay at the airport with you. Mummy's insane when it comes to Greek things — like it's such a big deal if I miss one summer school class. Do you hate me?"

I shake my head even though I know she can't see me. "Don't worry about it. It's fine. Really."

"Okay, but you hate Mummy, right? You do, don't you? You can tell me the truth now that we're home. I can handle it."

I stand up, struggling to keep my balance on my good foot. As tempted as I am to vent about Mrs. P, I like Kat too much to tell her the truth. "No, of course I don't hate her. In fact, with all the junk that went wrong on this trip, I needed someone like your mom to take care of me." I sigh into the phone. I don't want to talk about Mrs. P anymore. "So how was your flight back with Nick?" I ask, trying to change the subject.

There's an awkward pause on the line. "It was fine," she finally says. "Why wouldn't it be?"

I don't know why, but Kat's voice sounds defensive. I choose my next words carefully. "It's just that you've been acting a bit strange around him lately. Like you're annoyed with him or something."

"No, I'm fine. Really."

Her words don't match up with the tone of her voice. I exhale hard into the phone. "Look, Kat. I can tell something's bothering you. Are you totally, completely sure you don't want him for yourself? Because if you do ..." My voice trails off as I try to figure out the ending to that sentence. Would I break up with Nick if Kat wanted me to? Maybe. Probably. Gosh, I don't know.

"Would you stop it?" she says. "I've told you already a million times, I'm not interested in Nick. Okay?"

This time, the words definitely match up with the voice. Relief melts over me like sugar on hot cereal. "Okay, sorry. I just want to be sure." I hobble over to my nightstand so I can read the bright red numbers of my alarm clock. 9:37. I want to call Nick before it gets too late.

"Now we still have to figure out what to do about the Evil Eye," she says. "I think you should talk to Mummy —"

No. Not this again. "It's getting late, Kat," I cut in. "I've got tons of unpacking to do. Plus my parents want the deets on my trip. Can we talk about this another time?" But I don't really mean that. This is just one of those things we're never going to see eye to eye on. How can I make her understand that? I open my wallet to search for the scrap of paper where I wrote Nick's cell number.

Kat's voice in my ear turns serious. "No. This is important, Dani. It really can't wait."

I smile as I find the number tucked behind my credit card. "Okay, talk to you later," I say, guilt pinging my conscience as I click the phone off. I don't want to talk about silly superstitions anymore.

I want to call Nick.

Chapter 13
• • • • • • •

As much as I loved Greece, it feels good to be back in Toronto again. Before I left, Mom said something about how maybe I'd "start to appreciate the little luxuries of home" after I went away for a while. I hate to admit it, but she was so right. It feels great to be sleeping in my own bed, eating Timbits for breakfast, and, of course, taking freshwater showers again (the saltwater showers at the Olympic Palace were brutal on my hair). But definitely the best part about being home is getting my freedom back. Poor Kat. I don't know how she copes with her mother and her ever-watchful eye.

Two nights after our return, Nick comes over to meet my parents. They have this rule that I'm not allowed to go out with any boy they haven't met. It goes perfectly, of course. Nick shakes their hands and says all the right things. He's probably every parent's dream. Even my sisters seem charmed by him.

Because my ankle still isn't completely healed yet, he insists we should do something that doesn't require much walking. So we end up going for dessert at a local neighbourhood restaurant with candles on every table and frescoed walls. We order milkshakes and split a piece of chocolate cake. My stomach is turning somersaults just seeing him again, so it's hard to eat much. But of course, I don't tell *him* about the somersaults. I'm kind of surprised at how much I've missed him. After all, it's only been three days since we left Greece. But it feels like ages.

It's nice being with him here in Toronto, dressed in regular city clothes instead of bumming on the beach in our bathing suits. After dessert, we walk a bit around the neighbourhood. When my ankle gets sore, he lifts me up and carries me piggyback, which is cute and kind of romantic. Kat would freak out if she could see us. It's just like something out of one of her books.

Nick ends up piggybacking me all the way back to my driveway. He lowers me down gently until we're both standing beside Rosie (who's normally parked inside the garage, so I guess Dad must have left her outside after taking her for a spin today). And then Nick turns around and puts a hand around my shoulder just as a warm summer breeze ruffles through the leaves of the giant spreading maple tree on my front lawn. A whispery serenade.

"You have a new freckle," he says, touching his fingers to my cheek. A crop of goosebumps rises up over my bare arms. He's staring at me with the most mysterious smile on his face.

"There's something I want to give you." His voice is raspy — like there's a popcorn husk stuck in his airway. That's when I notice his right hand is tucked behind his back. My heart floats up into my mouth.

"What is it?"

"No, close your eyes first."

I squeeze them shut. I'm so curious, I almost forget to breathe.

"Now give me your hand."

I reach my right hand out slowly and wait. A second later, I feel his warm, slightly calloused fingers brushing across my arm. I can't help shivering — his touch is still like an electric shock against my skin.

"Okay, you can look now," he says after a minute.

My eyes fly open to see what he's given me. There, snaking across my wrist, is a thin rope of twisted silver wires. I bring my hand closer to my face, peering at the gift through the dim light of the streetlamp. "Oooh, it's beautiful, Nick," I say quickly, careful not to hurt his feelings with anything less than enthusiasm. But just between you and me, I'm having a hard time figuring out what's so special about a bracelet made out of wires.

"I made it for you from some of my electric guitar strings," he explains. His voice is barely louder than a whisper, like I'm a deer he might scare away by speaking too loudly. "I just wanted to give you something to let you know how much you mean to me. Music is my life and … uh, I wanted to share a piece of that with you."

Yeah. Now the bracelet really *is* beautiful. I twirl the silver wires around my wrist, inspecting the neatly finished ends and the perfect symmetry of the design. "I can't believe it. You really made this?" My eyes rise up to find his. It's hard to tell through the dark, but it looks like he's blushing. I open my mouth to speak but nothing comes out. For the first time in my life, I don't know what to say. This bracelet is probably one of the nicest things anyone's ever given me. Tears spring to my eyes, but I blink them away before they can show.

Nick clearly doesn't know what to make of my silence. "You don't have to wear it if you don't want," he says with a shake of his head. "It was just an idea …"

"No, I want to wear it," I insist, clamping my hand over the bracelet so he can't change his mind and take it back. "It's perfect, Nick. Thank you." I throw my arms around his neck and pull him close. "I'll wear it forever," I whisper into his ear.

"I'm happy," he says, and I feel his body relax against mine.

I really want to say more. I want to tell him how much he means to me and how I've never met anyone like him before and how I think I'm really and truly falling in love for the first time in my life. But I don't know how to say that to him. And somehow, I don't think I have to. Wearing his bracelet says it all.

Yeah, things are definitely starting to look up for me again. Nick and I are taking our relationship to the next level, my ankle's healing nicely, and I have a few weeks left to get my tan perfect before high school starts in September.

Bye-bye, Evil Eye, I think with a laugh.

But the very next morning, all my happiness goes down the toilet.

I wake up to the sound of yelling. Well, actually it's more like screaming. My mother screaming, to be specific. I wrap my pillow around my ears, trying to muffle the noise. My mother screaming at one of us isn't so unusual. I'm just happy her irritation isn't directed at me this time. *Wonder which of my sisters is in trouble?* I think, squeezing my eyes shut and hoping to slip back to sleep.

But then, through the silk of my pillowcase, I hear *my* name in the screams.

"Dani! Dani!"

My eyelids flip open and my head pops up like a jack-in-the-box. My thoughts skitter back over the past couple of days, trying to figure out what I possibly might have done wrong. *Maybe she found the chocolate stain I accidentally spilled on the suede purse I "borrowed" from her closet last night.* Just as I'm trying to formulate a good excuse, I hear the screen door slam and then the yelling suddenly goes blurry.

"Dani ... down right ... oh my ... been attacked!"

What? Attacked? Who? I spring out of bed and fly down the stairs as fast as my sore ankle will allow. My throat's suddenly thick with a growing sense of panic. "Mom? Dad? What's going on?" I manage to gasp, my throat closing over the words.

But when I get downstairs, there's no one there. I hobble frantically from room to room until I finally notice the front door hanging halfway open, as if someone left in a hurry. I limp outside to see my entire family standing in the driveway, each of their mouths pursed in a perfect circle of shock. I do a quick head count — Mom, Dad, Toby, and Charley. All of them are there. And none of them are bleeding to death. I want to cry with relief. "You scared me!" I pant. "What's all that screaming ab—"

I shut up when I see Toby raise her arm and silently point to Rosie. I follow the direction of her finger until I see it. That's when I start to scream too. Cute little Rosie has been attacked! Someone's slashed her tires, dissected her convertible top, and ripped up her beautiful red paint with their key. Rosie's completely and utterly ruined.

My knees buckle from the shock. Thankfully, Dad runs over and catches me before I hit the pavement. "It's okay. It's just a car," he says in my ear, pulling me back to my feet. "We'll call the police and they'll find who did this."

He tries to turn me the other way, but I resist. As horrible as it is, I just can't tear my eyes away from the ruined mess on my driveway. *What kind of sicko would do something like this?*

"It must have happened while we were sleeping," I hear one of my sisters say.

"At least the other cars weren't hurt," says the other. I think it's the other.

"Are you all right, Dani?" someone else asks. Probably Mom, but I'm not sure. I'm having a hard time focusing on their voices because Thalia's words of warning are pounding through my brain louder than a cranked-up bass line.

Beauty attracts a lot of attention — both good and bad. Be careful.

My head's spinning overtime as my brain makes the connection. *This is what she was talking about that night on the beach after Costa tried to kiss me. It's the same thing Kat has been trying to tell me about that Evil Eye thing. Oh God, I am cursed. They were both right all along.*

"Danz?" This time it's my father's voice speaking to me. And I can feel his arms tighten around my waist, shoring me up so I won't fall again. "I'm so sorry, I should have parked Rosie in the garage last night. But don't be sad. It's going to be okay. We'll get her fixed."

I shake my head, trying to swallow the sickening lump of fear that's rising in my throat. This bad luck is getting out-of-control scary. If something like this can happen to Rosie, there's no way of telling what other terrible things are coming my way. Or my family's, or my friends' … or Nick's. I stare at the shredded car in front of me. Everyone I love is potentially in danger. I have to do something to get rid of this curse. And I have to do it fast.

Next thing I know, Mom's taking my hand and leading me back into the house. "We better call the police. I'm sure they'll want to take some photos. Maybe even comb the car for evidence. Come inside, Dani, before you catch a cold. This isn't Greece, you know."

I look down and notice for the first time that I'm wearing nothing but a T-shirt and a faded pair of Little Miss Giggles underwear. Pulling the tee down to cover my behind, I follow Mom inside the house. Tears sting the backs of my eyelids as I hobble back up to my room and dig my phone out from under the pile of clothes on my floor. My hand's shaking as my thumb skips over the dial pad. Luckily, Kat answers on the first ring.

"Hey, can I come over?" I say, trying hard to keep my voice from breaking. "I need to talk to you. Like, now."

Chapter 14

• • • • • • •

Toby drives me to the Papadakises' house in her car. "I hope the police catch whoever did this," she says as we turn onto Kat's street. "The thought of some psychopath prowling around our street is just so creepy. I mean, I don't know what kind of weapon this guy was using, but we're lucky he didn't kill us all in our sleep."

I clutch my twisting stomach. I was too nauseous to eat any breakfast this morning. Lowering my window, I lean my head out and take a gulp of fresh air. It helps calm the queasiness a bit. "Can we just talk about something else now, please?"

But as usual, my sister doesn't listen to a word I say. "Strange how there wasn't even a scratch on the other cars, huh?" she continues. "I just wonder why yours was singled out? Maybe the guy only gets violent around the colour red."

"Yeah, maybe," I murmur, closing my eyes. I can't bring myself to tell Toby the truth: that my pretty face has made me the target of a centuries-old Greek curse. The whole thing is still kind of unbelievable to me, so I can only imagine how it would sound to her. And then she'll probably go tell Charley about it and together they'll spend the rest of the summer making my life even more heinous than it already is. Over the years, those two have become skilled masters of the whole little sister put-down routine. The last thing I need right now is to give them any more ammunition to use against me.

I stay silent for the rest of the ride. Kat meets me at the door and takes me straight upstairs to her bedroom. She shuts the door to give me some privacy. I start pacing frantically back and forth across her floor. I'm so tense right now, moving is the only thing that's keeping me calm.

"Did something else happen?" she asks. Her voice is hushed and ready. Like she knows something awful is coming.

"Yeah," I say weakly. "Just like you warned me it would."

"What is it?"

But just as I'm about to tell her about Rosie, something catches my eye. I stop pacing for a second and pick up a thick book balancing on the edge of her desk. The cover is all black except for the blood red letters of the title: *Curses and Cures*. The top edge of the book is littered with dog-eared corners, like someone's been reading it carefully and taking notes. I open it up and flip through the pages. The musty smell of old ink and stale paper breezes under my nose.

I turn to look at Kat, holding the book up to show her. My hand is trembling from all the stress. "What's this? I thought you said you weren't superstitious?"

"I'm *not* superstitious," she says, taking the book from me and tossing it back down on the desk. Real fast. Like she'll get cooties if she touches it too long. "It's my mother's book. She must have left it in my room. Now will you please tell me what happened before I die of suspense?"

My thoughts switch back to poor ruined Rosie. A sob flies out of my mouth and I bring my hands up to cover my face. I can feel tears coming, and it isn't going to be pretty. I hate crying in front of other people but this time it's completely unavoidable. At least it's just Kat. She's seen me at my worst.

"You were right," I say, collapsing onto her bed. "I'm cursed! If I'd only listened to you when you tried to warn me, Rosie would be okay right now."

"What do you mean? What happened to Rosie?"

The awful story comes pouring out in a swell of tears. When Kat hears what happened, she lets out a short shriek. After a minute, she pulls a box of tissues down from her bookshelf and comes over to sit beside me on the bed. "Wow, this is a really bad case," she says, handing me the box. "That girl on the beach must have been a witch or something."

I wipe my cheeks with the tissue as my thoughts careen back to that day in Greece and that strange little girl with her cold blue eyes. Kat has a point. It was right after our walk on the beach that everything started to go wrong for me. First the bad fish, then the sprained ankle, then the fiasco with my passport. And now poor Rosie.

"Hang on," I say, thinking back. "What about Costa? I saw

him that morning too. And he definitely looked at me funny. Kind of like this."

I raise one eyebrow up while trying to squint the other one down at the same time, just like Costa did that day. But I guess I'm not as good with impersonations as Kat. "Well, it was way scarier when he did it." I shrug. "And that day on the beach wasn't the only time." My mind flashes back to that night he tried to kiss me and a shudder creeps over my skin. *You'll be sorry*, he said.

Yeah, he could totally be the one who cursed me.

Kat flicks her bangs out of her eyes and sighs. "I don't think it matters who gave it to you. The important thing is to figure out how to cure it."

Her words are like mac and cheese to my ears. "Yes," I yelp, grabbing her hands and squeezing. "I want to get cured today. Before something even worse happens!" I let go of her hands and jump to my feet. "Where do we start?"

She gets up too. Marches over to the door, motioning for me to follow. "Mummy's downstairs. We have to ask her. She's an expert on the Evil Eye. I promise you, she'll know how to fix this."

We find her mother in the kitchen baking a batch of cookies. *So that's why this house smells like Christmas in the middle of the summer*, I think. There's half a pan full of perfectly shaped round sugar cookies spread out in tidy rows on the baking sheet beside her. The rest of the dough is still in a big lump and she's busily pounding and squeezing it into submission. It must be hard work because she's grunting with exertion. In fact, Mrs. P is concentrating so hard on her dough, she doesn't even notice us come in. She gives a startled jump when Kat comes up behind her and taps her on the shoulder.

"Ah!" she yelps, spinning around. "Oh, Katerina, you scared me!"

"Sorry, Mummy, but this is really important. You were right about the Evil Eye." She puts her arm around me and pulls me forward. "Dani's bad luck is getting worse. Someone attacked her car last night right in her own driveway."

Mrs. P gasps and drops her dough. When she turns towards me, her eyes are wide with shock. Practically as big as those sugar cookies. After a moment, she wipes her floury hands on her apron and pulls up a chair at the kitchen table. With a nod to me and Kat, she motions for us to sit too. She puts a dish of cookies in front of us and waits for us to take one. I do. It's buttery and sweet and it melts on my tongue like a snowflake.

"This news doesn't surprise me," she sighs, reaching across the table to take my hand. "Beauty can be a curse. And a girl as beautiful as you, Daniella, is a natural target for *Matiasma* — the Evil Eye."

I wait for her to let go of my hand. Although her skin smells of sweet, fresh butter, it's all rough and scratchy — like a gnarled old tree branch. And there are tiny red cuts all over her knuckles. *Who knew baking was such a workout?*

"I don't understand, Mrs. Papadakis. I never hurt anyone. So why would someone want to hurt me?"

She smiles a sad smile. "Whoever gave you this curse might not have intended to harm you. Usually the Evil Eye is completely involuntary. Let me tell you a story. In Greece, a grandmother is called *yiayia*. When my Yiayia was a young woman, she had three daughters — each of them born seven years apart. My own mother was the oldest of the three daughters. When she and her middle sister had grown into big girls and gone off to school, my Yiayia was left to spend her days with her youngest daughter, a pretty girl with soft brown curls, almond-shaped eyes, and a rosebud mouth. Every day, she liked to take her young daughter down to the village to go shopping for their daily food. One day, a stranger came to the village, saw the little girl, and said, 'What a beautiful child! She must make you so happy.' Well, my Yiayia was so proud of her child that she forgot to start spitting and denying the stranger's words."

I wince at that. *More spitting? What's with this family?*

"Almost immediately, the Evil Eye began to take effect," Mrs. P continues, her grip on my hand tightening as she names the curse. "The girl became ill overnight with a terrible stomach bug. She became dehydrated very quickly and, although the doctors tried everything to cure her, within two days, she was dead. Nothing could be done to save her life."

"All because of a stomach bug?" I gasp. "Like the one I had in Greece?"

Kat and her mother nod, their heads bobbing up and down in almost perfect synchrony. I'm amazed by how similar they look in that one moment. *When Kat grows up, she's going to look just like her mother,* I think. *Only hopefully not so constipated.* Then Mrs. P puts her other butter-scented hand over mine.

"You see? The child's beauty brought on the curse. Wealth and good fortune bring it on as well. The stranger didn't mean to harm the child, but her admiration for the little girl's beauty was deadly."

Her calloused palm scratches against mine like a brick of sandpaper. I can't take it any longer. Holding her scratchy hand is worse than listening to my parents sing karaoke.

"Okay, I totally get that this is a Greek thing," I say, pulling my hand away and sneaking it into my lap where she can't reach for it again. "But *I'm* not Greek. Why is this happening to me?"

Mrs. P holds a finger up in front of my face and waggles it back and forth like a metronome. "Daniella, *Matiasma* is not just for Greeks. There are many cultures that know and believe in the power of the Evil Eye." She counts on her fingers as she names off a list. "Morocco, Spain, Israel, Turkey, Russia, Iran, Italy. It's only here in the West that people are ignorant of the danger — walking around like peacocks, showing off their fancy things, flashy cars, giant homes, foolishly inviting the Evil Eye into their lives."

She looks angry. Like she's spraying poison along with the words flying from her lips. Suddenly, I begin to feel guilty. Did I bring this on myself? My thoughts zoom back to poor Rosie — demolished in my very own driveway. How I loved riding in my car and showing her off. Am I one of those peacocks she's talking about?

Mrs. P waves her hands at Kat. "Run and get my jewellery box. There should be something inside to help Daniella."

Jumping to her feet, Kat scurries up the stairs to fetch the box. I let out a big sigh of relief and slump back against the hard wooden chair. I'm already beginning to feel better.

Mrs. P has something to cure me. It's all going to end here.

She sits quietly, watching me eat another cookie, waiting to wash my dish. A minute later, Kat comes clomping down the stairs. I turn to see her walk into the kitchen holding a large box covered in a skin of fraying sky blue leather. She hands the box to her mother, as carefully as if she's passing her a newborn baby. Placing it gently on the table, Mrs. P lifts the lid. I can hear the small metal hinges creaking from exertion as a musty odour rises up and overtakes the lovely Christmas smell of the kitchen. *That thing must be ancient,* I think, trying to peek around the raised lid to see what's in there, but Mrs. P's hands block my view.

"Ah, yes. Here it is," she whispers as she reaches inside. I hold my breath while I wait to see what she has to cure me. A cute pair of earrings? A pendant? A little beaded bracelet like hers and Kat's? But what she pulls out of there makes me recoil in horror.

What is that thing?

"This necklace once belonged to my Yiayia," Mrs. P explains, her pinched lips spreading into a tight smile. "After the death of her daughter, she became a rabid believer in the Evil Eye. She crafted this necklace to keep it away. My Yiayia passed this to my mother when she was pregnant with my older sister, Sophia."

"You know, the same Sophia we stayed with in Greece," whispers Kat, in case I'm not following closely enough.

Mrs. P nods. "That's right. My sister passed it on to me when I became pregnant with Katerina to help protect our house from the curse. My Yiayia had the reputation of being the most super-stitious woman on our island. The power of this necklace was once legendary in our part of Greece. My mother used to tell us that it was the strongest amulet ever created to keep *Matiasma* away."

Bringing the thing to her lips, she kisses it and then holds it for me to take.

I stare at her in shock. That thing isn't a necklace. Necklaces are beautiful, dainty, delicate things that help show off a woman's beauty. What she's holding out to me is like something straight out of a horror movie. A big, ugly string of giant blue glass eyeballs. *She doesn't actually expect me to wear it, does she?*

Because I don't know what else to do, I take the thing between my thumb and forefinger and, with my arm stretched out as far as it'll go, slowly examine it. "How exactly does a bunch of eyeballs keep this curse away, Mrs. P?" I don't want to be rude. But, as much as I try, it's just impossible to keep the horror from creeping into my voice.

With a sigh, Mrs. P stands up, grabs the thing from me, and loops it around my head. I shiver as the glass eyeballs come in contact with the bare skin of my neck. It's heavy and clunky and cool to the touch.

"Don't you see?" she demands, her words short with frus-tration. "If someone looks at you with the Evil Eye, *these* eyes deflect the curse away from you."

I'm suddenly overwhelmed by the awful feeling that my life is spinning out of control. More than anything, I want to tear this disgusting thing off me and fling it across the room. I want to tell this lady that her superstitions are stupid. I want to tell her that I wish I'd never gone with her to Greece ... that I should have stayed here where people don't do curses. And necklaces are pretty. And beauty isn't something to be feared.

But all that will probably just make her mad.

And then maybe she won't help me anymore.

And I *really* need her help.

But the necklace is *so* ugly.

I bite my lip and shift in my seat as I wonder what to say. Mrs. P's eyes narrow. "Daniella, if you're serious about removing this curse, you'll stop pouting and accept this gift."

That's when I realize I don't have much choice. This necklace is the lesser of the two evils. Literally. My stomach lurches as I force out the most grateful smile I can muster. "Thanks, Mrs. P. I — I appreciate your help."

Her face softens. But just a bit. "You're welcome. I want you to be safe."

And with that, she closes the lid of the jewellery box with a soft thump and goes back to her cookies. Clearly, I've been dismissed. Kat walks me to the door. The necklace thuds against my chest with every step I take. No kidding, it feels like it weighs about fifty pounds.

"So, do you feel better now? I told you Mummy would know what to do."

"Kind of, I guess." Should I tell Kat how I really feel? Will she be hurt if she knows how much I despise her mother's necklace? "It's just so ... big. And freaky." I catch a glimpse of myself in the hall mirror and shudder. All those eyeballs hanging off the string are giving me the creeps.

"Yeah, but it's going to work. Just don't take it off. Not even when you're sleeping. You heard Mummy — she said this is really powerful. Wear it every day and, I'm telling you, your luck will change."

"I really hope you're right," I reply. The image of my poor, ruined Rosie flashes through my head again. At this point, I'd probably wear a string of *real* eyeballs if it would keep this bad luck away. I don't want to think about what — or who — this curse might hurt next.

"Just do me a favour, Kat? Don't tell Nick about this. I don't want him to, you know, freak out or anything. We're really starting to get serious." I hold out my guitar string bracelet for her to see. "Look what he made me."

Kat's eyes grow wide as she inspects the bracelet. "Yeah, that Nick's a great guy." Then she smiles and gives my shoulder a squeeze. "Don't worry, Dani. Your secret's safe with me."

Chapter 15

· · · · · · ·

Luckily, I've been able to hide the eyeball necklace pretty well under some lightweight turtlenecks and high-necked sweaters. Yeah, it's August, but I don't mind sweating a bit if it means keeping it a secret. So far I haven't taken it off for a second. Not even in the shower. Not even overnight, even though it's been ruin-ing my sleep. No matter what position I try or how many pillows I use, it pokes into me all night long. I have the bruises all over my neck and chest to prove it.

On my date with Nick tonight, I figure out a way to hide it under one of Mom's silk scarves. He's invited me to his house to watch a movie. That has me feeling nervous and excited at the same time.

"His parents will be home, right?" Mom asked when I told her about my plans.

"Of course," I replied, although I'm not really sure. I kind of hope they are, though. It would be nice to meet them.

Now I'm standing on his doorstep, checking my reflection in the mirror of my compact. Luckily, the necklace is still perfectly hidden by the scarf. I tuck the mirror back in my purse. When he opens the door, his smile greets me like a sunrise.

"Are your mom and dad here?" I ask, peeking around his shoulders for signs of parental activity.

Now Nick looks sheepish. "Sorry, they're out at a party. We're here alone."

I hesitate in the doorway. He notices. "That okay? I could call Mrs. P if you'd feel better with a chaperone."

I giggle at that. "No, thanks." I walk through, feeling even more nervous and excited than before. I'm hoping he won't discover the awful necklace. As long as he doesn't get too close to me, I should be fine.

After the movie, Nick gets me a glass of ice water and takes me downstairs to show me his room. Okay, I admit that I wondered about his bedroom. But it turns out to be way more impressive than anything I imagined. When he flicks on the lights, I see that the entire basement has been converted into a bedroom/music studio. Every wall is covered in vintage rock and roll posters featuring dudes with shaggy hair, electric guitars, platform shoes, and bell-bottom pants. Across from his desk, there's a complete drum set, a stage, a sound system, and a whole lineup of guitars. I pluck a string on the shiny electric one at the end of the line, smiling because it reminds me of my Nick bracelet. Putting down my glass of water, I pick up the only acoustic one in the bunch and hold it out to him.

"Play a song for me?"

Nick laughs. "I can't. They're all bass guitars."

Am I supposed to understand what that means? "They're instruments, right? Don't they make music?"

"Yes. But just the bass line. There's no melody."

Okay. Still don't know what he's talking about. "Come on," I plead. "You're telling me with all these guitars, you can't play me one song?"

He holds up his hands in surrender. "Okay, fine. You win." He takes the guitar from me and throws the strap over his shoulder. "I'll play 'Under Pressure.' It's an old song, but somebody did a cover of it a few years ago so you might know it."

I have to stop myself from laughing as he picks out the tune. "Under Pressure." He has absolutely no way of knowing how perfectly that describes my life these days. And I'm determined to do everything I can to keep it that way. I sit down on the edge of his bed and listen to the easy, low tones of his bass.

"How long have you been playing?"

Nick looks up from the guitar and grins. He's to-die-for cute when he smiles. It actually hurts my eyes to look at him sometimes. "Since before I can remember. My mom says that even as a baby, I always chose instruments over toys. She has pictures of me playing Dad's guitar on the floor when I was too small to lift it."

I make a mental note to ask Mrs. Barbas to show me some of those baby pictures when I meet her. When the song's over, he puts the guitar back on its stand and comes to sit beside me on the edge of the bed. His eyes lock with mine as he circles his arms around my shoulders and pulls me close. I tense with nerves. Any closer and he'll discover Mrs. P's awful necklace. And then he'll know about the curse.

"It's getting late. I think I should get going," I say, pushing him away before he can hug me. I jump to my feet and step away from the bed. My hands fly up to my neck, checking to see if the scarf is still in place. Nick looks surprised at my reaction. But thankfully, he doesn't argue.

"Okay. I'll walk you home now." I can tell by the sound of his voice that he's disappointed.

I hate having to push him away. But what choice do I have?

Overnight, Toronto gets hit with a late-summer heat wave. When I open my window, I practically choke on the air. I'm talking "fry an egg on the sidewalk" type weather. Turtlenecks and silk scarves are suddenly out of the question. What am I going to wear now? No way I'm going to be able to hide my eyeball necklace under a T-shirt or a tank top. I run my fingertips over one of the smooth glass balls wondering what to do. I consider taking it off. But it's still too early to know if it's been helping or not. Nothing bad has happened to me in five days — the longest stretch of time since this whole mess started. *Does that mean I'm cured?* Feeling brave, I pick it off my neck and lift it up to my forehead. I pause and wait, for what I don't know. A lightning bolt? A clap of thunder? The roof to come crashing down over my head?

Despite the heat outside, a cool shiver runs up my back. I drop the necklace back down with a thump. No, I should keep wearing it until I'm sure the bad luck is gone. Really and truly gone. Just a couple more days. I take a deep breath and head downstairs to the kitchen.

"Dude. Why are you wearing that disgusting thing around your neck?" Toby asks, walking in halfway through my bowl of Lucky Charms.

Putting down my spoon, I close my eyes, take a deep breath, and swallow the urge to reply with something snarky. "It's just something Mrs. Papadakis gave me," I say, oh so calmly. "This necklace belonged to her grandmother."

"Okay. But that still doesn't explain why you're actually wearing it."

I'm trying to protect you and the rest of this family from getting slashed to pieces in the middle of the night, like what happened to Rosie, I feel like yelling. "It's supposed to keep bad luck away," I say instead. Toby snorts and chugs a glass of orange juice.

"And you think *that* thing is going to help? It looks like a prosthetic eye factory threw up all over you."

Now Charley joins us at the breakfast table. I brace myself for the worst. "It's hideous. It makes you look like a freak," she chimes in.

Okay, that's it. I push my chair away from the table. "Very helpful. Thanks."

I can hear them laughing as I storm out of the room. I feel like clocking both of my sisters with my string of giant eyeballs.

Why exactly am I trying so hard to keep them from getting killed? It's easy to forget when they treat me this way. Maybe I should just be happy it's taken them this long to notice the necklace. After all, I've been wearing the stupid thing for almost a week now.

Nick calls shortly after breakfast. "Want to come over for a swim? It's going to be a scorcher."

Yes, yes, yes, I want to shout.

"I don't think so," I say instead. "My, um, cousins are visiting from out of town. I have to spend the day with them."

Can he tell I'm lying? My conscience pings with guilt. But what choice do I have? There's no hiding this necklace under a bathing suit. Nick's Greek too, which means he probably believes in the Evil Eye. And once he sees my string of eyeballs, he'll know I'm cursed. And then for sure he won't want anything to do with me anymore.

I can't take the chance.

"Cousins?" Nick asks. "You never mentioned them before. Can't you get away for a bit? I really want to see you."

His voice sounds gruff. I picture the sad pout look that's probably on his face and feel even worse. Man, I hate lying to him. But what can I do? What would you do if you were in my shoes?

"Sorry, I really can't leave them," I mumble. "My parents made these plans for us a long time ago and I can't bail on them now. I'll have more time next week, I promise."

Because hopefully by then, I'll be rid of this curse, I think. I hope. I pray. Honestly, I don't know how long I'm going to keep this act up. At this point, I feel like I'm at the end of my rope.

Turns out, I'm going to need a bit more rope.

I go shopping with Mom that afternoon, hoping it'll help me de-stress. We finish with a mani-pedi at the day spa around the corner. When we get home, we find the front door of our house coated in a layer of dripping eggs and a carpet of shattered shells strewn across our porch. Mom and I stand in the driveway and watch the oozing mess in silence. My heart is a block of concrete.

"Should we call the police?" I finally ask.

Mom shakes her head and sighs. "No. It's probably just some neighbourhood kids playing a stupid prank. I'm going to walk around the house and make sure nothing else has been damaged."

I'm too upset to go with her. Instead, I pull out my phone and send a text to Kat: <911—EE still here>

Without a thought for my freshly painted toenails, I crunch through the mess of broken shells, unlock the dripping door, and limp right up to my room to wait for a reply. A few minutes later, "Get Lucky" goes off in my purse. I fumble to answer it. Before I can even say hello, Kat's words rush into my ear.

"We need a new plan. Mummy says that the necklace might not be the answer."

I almost drop the phone. "Excuse me?"

"She says it's definitely helpful if you want to keep the Evil Eye away *before* the curse has been made. But since you're already cursed, it's probably not doing much. You can take it off now. She has another idea. Something a bit more drastic."

Are you kidding me? I yank the thing off my neck and toss it to the floor. "What is it?" I ask, pulling in a deep breath and trying to prepare myself for what's coming next. Somehow, I know I'm not going to like it.

"She wants to know if you have any garlic in your kitchen. You'll need at least three pieces."

What a bizarre question. "I don't know. Why?"

"Mummy says a good way to ward off the Evil Eye is to carry garlic in your pockets. It has to be the real stuff — garlic powder doesn't count."

"Isn't garlic for vampires?"

"Yeah. But it works for evil spirits too."

"But I'll stink."

Kat sighs. She sounds frustrated. "Maybe a bit. But it won't be forever. Mummy says evil spirits hate the smell of garlic. It's a really effective way to send them packing."

Yeah, and everyone else in my life too. I can hear my words morphing into a whine. "You don't seriously expect me to do this, do you, Kat?"

Her voice hums with pity. "It shouldn't be for long. Just until your luck turns around again. Then we'll know that the Evil Eye is gone for good."

I let out a tortured sigh as I trudge down the stairs to search the fridge for garlic. *What am I going to do about Nick? How on earth am I going to explain my new odour to him?* I can't help but wonder which would be a bigger turnoff — the garlic or the curse? One thing's for sure, I don't want to find out. I'll just have to keep avoiding him. But for how long? A week? Two?

How much longer will he wait around for me? What if the garlic doesn't work? Then what?

I decide not to think about that possibility. *This has to work,* I tell myself as I locate an abandoned bunch of garlic at the back of the fridge. I tear it apart and find six cloves inside. Kat says that three cloves will be enough. Maybe for anybody else, that would be fine. But I'm desperate. If three cloves are good, six will be even better. As per Kat's instructions, I peel them and stick them all over my clothes. One in each pocket, one tucked into my underwear, two in my T-shirt pocket. I have one left over, so I put it in my mouth and swallow it, my lips twisting as I force it down. Now I'm ready to fight off the evil spirits with my own breath. I lean over and give my body a couple of sniffs but don't really smell anything. A tiny spark of hope rises up in my chest. Maybe this cure isn't going to be so bad after all?

But an hour later when my sisters get home from the mall, they dash that bit of hope to smithereens.

"Ew!" says Charley, waving a hand in front of her nose. "What's wrong with you?"

Toby backs away, her nose wrinkled like a bulldog. "You smell like a heap of garbage. No wonder people are egging our house. You're disgusting."

I indulge in a smile as I watch them leave the room. At least I know the garlic's working. If it can repel my dreadful sisters, those evil spirits don't stand a chance.

Now if I can just keep telling myself that, maybe it'll come true.

Nick calls again later that night.

"Come on, Dani, can't you just sneak out for a bit? I'm sure your family will understand. Remember how much fun we had the time we snuck out in Greece? And it's a clear night tonight — perfect to see the stars. I'll show you some new constellations."

My thoughts flash back to that night at the ruins. It's so tempting. "I'd love to," I start to say. But then I remember how my sisters reacted to my new, um, body odour. I don't want to go out with him smelling like a heap of garbage. "But I can't. I'm sorry."

His voice turns gruff again. "Not even for a bit?"

Shoot. Why is he making this so hard on me? "Sorry, but we're having a big dinner here tonight. You know how it is with family."

"Fine, then I'll come over there. I don't mind hanging out with your family if it means I get to see you."

My fingers twist nervous pretzel knots in my lap. "Please, Nick. Just one more week. Once my grandparents leave, we'll see each other every night. I promise."

The phone line goes deadly quiet.

This is where things really start to go downhill, you think.

"You said it was your *cousins* who were visiting," he finally says. His words are short and furry with frost. My face burns with a mortified heat. Is that the smell of garlic sizzling on my skin or just my sick imagination?

"Yeah. That's what I meant," I lie. "My cousins *and* my grandparents. They're actually all here."

But it's too late.

"Have a great night, Dani," he says. Before I can say another word, he hangs up.

Anger boils in my belly. I click off my phone and hurl it against the wall. It hits one of my little jewelled mirrors, shattering it into a spiderweb of broken glass. *Another sign of bad luck.* A crazy-sounding cackle flies out of my mouth as I stare at the ruined mirror. *Fine, go ahead,* I think, *add another seven years to my sentence.* At this point, I almost don't care.

Flinging open the door, I race out of my room and run outside into the hot night. My ankle throbs with each step as I stagger up the street. My head is spinning with so much self-pity that I can barely feel the pain. And my eyes are blurred with so many hot tears that I can't see straight. I don't even see the end of the sidewalk when I rush out into the street. And I definitely don't see the big black minivan that's heading straight for me.

BEEEEEEEEEEEEEEEP!!!!!

The horn blasts in my ears. My heart freezes in my chest as my eyes fly up to see two glowing headlights and a big black bumper screech to a stop just inches from my body. A second later, the angry driver sticks his head out the window. His mouth is a black pit.

"You're lucky you didn't just get killed, kid!"

Lucky? Seriously? Despite my racing heart, I actually laugh. And then I cry. Right there in public. I've never done that before. I must look terrible. But for the first time since I can remember, I don't care what I look like. *What on earth is happening to me?*

My face dripping with tears, I keep running down the street.

I have no idea where I'm going and I don't even care. I feel like I might actually be losing my mind. After a few minutes of blind running, I realize I'm heading south — the direction of Nick's house. But that's dumb — he won't want to see me now. Not after what just happened.

I spin around and run the other way — this time towards the Papadakises' house. But halfway there, I slow up. *What exactly are they going to be able to do for me? Give me another crazy cure? No thanks. I've had enough of those. Where else can I go? I can't get far on this ankle. And all of my other friends are still away at camp.*

My eyes foggy with tears, I begin to walk again. I really don't know how I find my way home. It's like there's a pair of invisible hands on my shoulders, steering me in the right direction. A few minutes later, I'm on my own front porch. The eggshells have been swept away, but I can still see the streaky outlines on the door where the broken yolks dripped down the glass. I dash right past them, straight upstairs, and lock myself in my room where the Evil Eye can't hurt me.

Maybe I should stay here for the rest of the summer. Maybe I should become one of those hermits who never go outside. Maybe I can live off the packs of gum and half-eaten snacks at the bottom of my purses. I have my TV to keep me company, after all.

Right?

Right.

Part of my brain realizes that I'm not thinking rationally. But a stronger, more desperate part of my brain has taken over.

Still crying, I stagger to my bathroom, pull the garlic cloves out of my clothes, and flush them down the toilet. Even then, the smell lingers. So I jump into the shower and wash my body three times with my watermelon body wash. When I come out and dry myself off, I can still smell the garlic.

Kat was right. That stuff *is* powerful. Too bad it didn't do a thing to help me. I crawl into my bed and pull the blanket over my head. I just want everything to be normal again. It's hard to believe that only a couple of weeks ago my biggest worry was getting a bad tan line.

Now it feels like I'm fighting for my life.

Chapter 16
· · · · · · ·

And so the next day, I turn to hermit-hood.

To be honest, the first couple hours aren't so bad. I cower under my covers, do some yoga breathing, and try my best to stay calm. But about halfway through the morning, the air in my room starts to get stuffy and the garlic smell becomes overpowering. Like, hard-to-breathe overpowering. I can't even open my window to get fresh air because I know the heat wave outside will turn my room into an oven. I go to my bathroom and spray on some perfume. But that just makes it worse. Now I smell like lilac-scented shrimp scampi.

Gross.

I crawl back into bed and try to ignore it. When I don't show up for breakfast, Mom must figure I'm sleeping in. But when I haven't made an appearance by lunchtime, she comes looking for me. It's about one-thirty when I hear her gel nails clicking against my door like a synthetic drum roll. That's how my mother knocks.

"Dani? Are you okay?"

I lift my head a couple of inches off the pillow. "I'm fine. I just want to be by myself today."

"Did something happen?"

Yeah, someone put an evil curse on me and I can't shake it.

"Honey? Do you want to talk?"

"No! I'm fine, really. Just leave me alone, please."

I breathe a sigh of relief when I hear her footsteps disappearing back down the hall. I settle down into a dreamlike trance. Not awake and not asleep. Just a loop of short, shallow breaths. The bare minimum for survival.

Later in the afternoon Mom's back rattling my doorknob. And this time, she's brought the Dreadful Duo with her. "Dani, can you unlock this door? We'd like to come in."

"No, thanks."

"Dani? Your sisters are here. They want to say something to you."

I poke my head out from under my covers and turn towards the door. What on earth do Toby and Charley want to say now? I hold my breath and listen. At first there's only silence. Then Toby's familiar voice, whining through the door, "Fine. Okay, okay ..."

Mom must have elbowed her.·

There's a sudden pounding of a fist against the wood. "Hey! Sorry I was mean to you. You're not disgusting. And you don't smell like a garbage heap."

And then more pounding, followed by Charley's voice. "Yeah, I'm sorry too."

I sit up in bed. My sisters are sorry? That has to be a first. For a moment, I consider opening the door and letting them in. And then I hear the unmistakable sound of Charley snickering into her hand. I should have known better.

"Dani? Did you hear that?" It's Mom again. "Your sisters are sorry. Can we come in now?"

I dive back under my blanket. "No!"

That does it. Now Mom's mad.

"Daniella Ryanne Price! If you don't unlock this door right now, I will call the police and have them tear it down!" She's screaming now. Told you she's a screamer.

"No!" I answer, calling her bluff. "This isn't about you or Toby or Charley. I just want to be alone!" I know she'll never call the police about something like this. She'll just wait for Dad to come home and let him handle it. Luckily for me, he doesn't usually get home 'til past dinnertime. Hopefully by then, Mom will have forgotten all about me.

A trio of footsteps stomp away down the hall. And then silence. Hours pass while I fade in and out of restless sleep. It's strangely quiet in the house. So quiet, I can hear my empty stomach rumble and roll. Finally, with a sigh, I glance at my clock: 4:16 p.m. My stomach growls again — louder this time. Gum doesn't take you far on an empty stomach. And I haven't found nearly as many half-eaten bags of chips at the bottom of my purses as I thought I would. Andrea, our cleaning lady, must have gone through my closet and cleared out some of my trash while I was away in Greece.

Just the thought of the chips makes my stomach moan. Trying

to ignore it, I pick up my cellphone to call Nick. Maybe my hunger's making me delusional, but I'm suddenly ready to tell him everything. If I confess about being cursed, maybe he'll understand why I lied about not seeing him.

I dial his number, but chicken out and hang up just before it starts to ring. What if he breaks up with me and says he never wants to see me again? Or even worse, what if he forgives me and then gets hit by a car on his way over here — the next victim of this curse? I'll never be able to forgive myself. Maybe the best thing to do is to just cut him loose. At least until my life goes back to normal again.

Chucking my phone into my closet, I dive back under the covers and try to ignore the waves of hunger that are crashing around in my stomach. Another hour ticks by. Just when I think the world might actually have given up on me, there's a knock at my door. A soft, timid knock. Definitely not my mother or my sisters. I glance at my clock again: 5:30. Too early for Dad to be home. For the tiniest of moments, my heart flickers with hope. "Nick?" I whisper under my breath, too scared to say his name out loud. But a girl's voice floats under the door instead.

"It's me. Kat."

My heart sinks. "I don't want to see anyone."

I hear a soft thud. Like a forehead bumping against the door. "Please can I come in? I think I understand why you're doing this. I'm here to help."

"How could you possibly understand?" I moan. "No one's put a curse on *you*."

She rattles the doorknob. "Listen, I have a list of ideas from Mummy. I'm going to stay with you until we get rid of this thing, okay? One of these ideas *has* to work."

"Excuse me, but what are you talking about?' Mom's outside my door too. And she's starting to scream again. "Get rid of what? Will someone please tell me what's going on?"

I feel the tears coming again. I've officially never cried this much in my life. Sliding off my bed, I shuffle through the mess on my floor and unbolt the door.

"Fine, Kat. But just you," I say, opening it up a crack. Ushering her inside, I push it shut quickly and turn the lock. She's only been in my room for a couple of seconds before my smell hits her. She struggles to keep the grimace of disgust off her face. But it doesn't work.

"I know I stink," I say with a shrug.

"It's not so bad," she lies. Then, as if to prove that she's telling the truth, she steps towards me and gives me a tight hug. I hug her back. She's so skinny, even when she's wearing a backpack, my arms feel like they're holding onto a stick.

"Why did you lock yourself in here?" she asks. "Your mother's really worried about you."

I let her go and stumble back to my bed. I must be getting light-headed from lack of food. "I'm not going to leave this room again," I whisper, in case Mom or my sisters are listening at the door. "It's not safe. Do you know I almost got flattened by a car last night?"

Her face scrunches with worry. She takes a seat at my desk

and pulls a small yellow notepad out of her backpack. "Cheer up. I've got a list of new ideas from Mummy. She read through that big book of curses and cures today. One of these will work for sure." And then she does the most perfect impersonation of Mrs. P's "sucking lemons" face. Despite my awful mood, I have to crack a smile.

"So," she continues, "the first thing on the list is a cure my Yiayia used to take whenever she thought that someone had given her the Evil Eye. It's pretty easy, so we can go do it right now. All we have to do is go to a Greek Orthodox church and ask the priest for some holy water."

The smile dies on my lips. "What for?"

"You'll have to drink it, of course. But only after I spit in it three times."

Stale potato chip crumbs rise up in my throat. "Are you kidding me?" I say. "What is it with all the spitting? It's disgusting."

"Of course I'm not kidding. Didn't you ever see that old movie *My Big Fat Greek Wedding*? Don't you remember when they spit on the bride? Spit scares the Evil Eye away. Everyone knows that."

I shake my head emphatically. "Your garlic cure was bad enough. Sorry, but there's no way on earth I'm going to drink spit. Don't even try to change my mind, 'cause it won't work. What's next on that list?"

With a sigh, Kat consults her notepad again. "Okay, you're probably not going to like the next one either, but Mummy's pretty sure it'll work. Although she's never tried this cure herself."

I lean forward, eager to hear. "I'm listening."

She's chewing on the corner of her lip. Like she'd rather be anywhere other than here right now.

"What is it?" I press.

Her voice lowers to a whisper. "Well, Mummy says that if you go back to Greece and gouge out the eyes of the girl who cast the spell, the curse will probably be lifted."

Narrowing my eyes, I look at her very carefully, trying to decide whether or not she's being serious. *Crap. I think she is.* A creepy feeling begins to tiptoe its way up my spine. I lower my voice another notch. "Are you and your mother insane?"

Kat's brown eyes widen with surprise. "No!"

"Good. Because I'm *not* gouging out anyone's eyes. I might be desperate, but not *that* desperate. And anyway, I don't know for sure it was that girl from the beach. Costa's a suspect too. What if I gouged out the wrong person's eyes? I can't believe I'm even discussing this. No, no — the answer is *no!*"

With a shake of her head, Kat picks up the list again and scans her eyes down the page. "There's one more thing on the list. It's probably the hardest. But, according to Mummy, definitely the most effective."

"What?" I demand.

Stepping carefully over my piles of dirty clothes, Kat crosses the room and takes a seat on the bed next to me. If she's still offended by my garlicky smell at all, she doesn't let on. "Mummy explained to me how the Evil Eye is all about jealousy. So she says that the fastest way to get rid of it is to give up everything in your life that other people might be jealous of."

I shrug as I look around my room. "Okay, like what?"

"She gave me a few suggestions for you." Kat looks back down at her list. "First of all, she said you shouldn't get Rosie fixed. That car has probably been attracting the Evil Eye from day one. And she also mentioned cutting your hair — it's too long and pretty. A shorter cut would be much better. And she also suggested that you go through your closet and pare it down. If you get rid of some of your fancy, expensive clothes and designer shoes and purses, people would stop looking at you. And then they wouldn't be jealous anymore. And then the Evil Eye would be gone forever."

My first reaction is another emphatic *no*. "Sorry. What else is on your list?"

That's when Kat puts down her notepad and shakes her head slowly. "Like I said, that was Mummy's last suggestion. There's nothing left."

No cures left? Really? "So you're telling me I have to choose between drinking spit, tracking down and mutilating a kid, or giving away my stuff?"

Kat just nods, her lips smashing together in a tight, thin line. Standing up, I walk over to my closet and look inside. Stacks of shoes, piles of clothes, rows of purses teeter on either side of me. My eyes skip across the various racks and shelves that line the walls. How much do I really care about these things anyway? Suddenly, the stuff fades away and my thoughts soar back to that day at the Greek airport when I didn't know if I was ever going to get home again. In those awful hours, all I wanted were my parents, my home, my bed. And yes, even my wicked sisters. I don't remember yearning for any of this stuff. Not even Rosie. Not even for a second. Clothes and shoes and purses and cars — these aren't the things that matter to me.

"Dani?"

At the sound of Kat's voice, the scene in front of me slowly eases back into focus. Man, there's a lot of junk in this closet. Does all this really belong to me? Why haven't I ever noticed how much of it there is before now? Maybe I'm like that Queen Cassiopeia from Greek mythology. Too vain and proud for my own good. And this is the universe's way of hanging me out to dry.

"Dani?"

"Yeah?" I say, still staring at my overflowing closet.

I hear the bedsprings creak as she rises off the mattress. "I think you should ask yourself, what good is all this stuff when you're too afraid to even step outside your own bedroom?"

Whoa. Good question. As I turn to answer, I catch a glimpse of myself in my shattered mirror. I rake a hand through my long hair and watch with horror as a grotesque, broken reflection of myself stares back. I look hideous. But I don't care. I, Dani Price, don't care how I look anymore. What the heck's happening to me? I don't even care about getting Rosie fixed. All I want is for the bad luck to go away. And if getting rid of all this stuff will lift the curse and make my life normal again, I'm ready to do it.

I turn away from the shattered mirror and walk over to Kat.
"I'll get the scissors," I say.

Chapter 17
• • • • • • •

Over the next few days, I go through everything I own and give away more than half of it. Belts I've never worn. Jackets I've forgotten I had. Purses I don't carry. Shoes that are out of style. Jewellery I never liked in the first place. Kat's thrilled to take it all off my hands, and I'm thrilled to let her have it. She's in desperate need of a new wardrobe anyway. With every box I cart over to her house, I feel a surprising change in myself. A feeling of lightness seems to come with owning less stuff. Does that mean the curse is lifting? I'm not exactly sure. But what I'm doing feels good. Like I'm taking the right steps to get my life back again.

I'm even getting used to my new haircut. I barely even care that it's so short and choppy. And with the heat wave we're having, the air on my neck is kind of refreshing. Mom, however, definitely doesn't agree. When I finally emerged from my room that night after I let Kat cut it, she was horrified. Her eyes bulged out and all the colour drained from her face. She looked like a vampire from one of those cheesy movies.

"Oh my God, look at you!" she shrieked, reaching out to touch my head. "What have you done?"

"Come on, Mom, it's only hair. Short is the style now anyway. It's very Miley Cyrus."

She started crying and clutching at her head. You'd think *she* was the one who lost her hair. "Why? Why, Dani?" she wailed, grabbing onto the wall for support. "I'll take you to the beauty parlour first thing in the morning — they'll fix it up so it won't be so bad. Maybe they can even put in some extensions."

But I refused. Honestly, the last thing I want in my life is more beauty. As far as I'm concerned, this is my last chance at ditching this curse and I'm not about to mess it up.

That was a whole week ago, and so far Mrs. P's plan seems to be working. Nothing bad has happened to me lately, and I'm actually beginning to think I'm in the clear. Of course, through it all, I've been missing Nick something awful. Has he been thinking about me? Is he still mad? Will he give me another chance? I'm aching to see him again and find out. Now that the bad luck's under control, I'm really hoping we can start all over. So when the day finally comes that Mrs. P declares me curse-free, I hop on my old bike and ride straight to his house. I'm so excited to see him, I practically pound down the front door. After a few seconds, a tall, beautiful woman with a side-swept bob and glowing green eyes answers. I clear my throat nervously. "Mrs. Barbas?"

"Yes? Can I help you?"

It's obvious where Nick gets his looks from. When she smiles, she looks just like him. Well, except for those tiny lines creasing out from the corners of her eyes. But somehow, this lady's able to make her wrinkles look good. "My name is Dani Price. Is Nick home?"

In an instant, her smile shrinks and those happy creases fade away. She leans against the door frame and cocks her head to one side, like she's studying me. I shift my weight from one foot to the other while I wait for her to say something. I feel like a bug under a microscope. My fantasy about looking over Nick's baby pictures with this woman dies a quick death right then and there. After the longest minute of my life, Mrs. Barbas finally nods and points towards the back of the house.

"He's in the pool. You can go right through." Her Greek accent is strong and reminds me of Mrs. P's, but I don't mention that. I have a feeling that the less I say, the better. "Thanks," I say simply, hurrying through the house before she can change her mind.

The pool sits in the middle of a beautiful cedar deck, surrounded by landscaped beds of brilliantly coloured flowers. Nick's alone in the water, face down, cutting gracefully through the blue water with his perfect front crawl. I watch him swim a few lengths — his arms paddling through the water, his skin glistening in the morning sunlight. Seeing him in his bathing suit instantly reminds me of our days in Greece. I miss our time there. More than anything, I want to jump right into the water, say I'm sorry, and wrap my arms around him.

But I don't.

So much has happened in the past few weeks. And somewhere along the way, I know I've lost the right to act like his girlfriend. So instead, I kneel down by the side of the pool and tap his shoulder as he swims towards me.

"Nick?"

He lifts his face out of the water and looks at me in surprise. I take a shaky breath and smile my signature smile. *Please, please, please let everything be okay.* For a second, he smiles back and my heart flickers with hope. But the smile disappears and the light in his eyes clouds over with anger. With a splash, he pushes away from the edge of the pool. "What?" he asks, his voice as cold as a dead fish.

My words feel thick in my throat — like a peanut butter sandwich that won't go down. "I wanted to see you. We never got a chance to talk about what happened last week."

He stands up so we're face to face and he rakes a hand through his dripping hair. My heart swells as I watch him. I take a deep breath and inhale a lungful of his coconut sunscreen. I think about Greece again. And how he told me I made a carnival happen inside his head. *All day, every day,* he said. The carnival can't be over, can it? Another flicker of hope sparks inside me. And then he gives his head a slow, sad shake and the spark dies out.

"Don't do this, Dani," he says. "Whatever we had, it's over now. Okay?"

My heart plummets into my flip-flops. *What? Just like that?* His words gut me so deeply, I almost lose my balance. *I can't believe I'm losing him after everything I've been through. I was so sure the curse was gone.*

I struggle to find my voice as I steady myself again. "It's over? But, I don't understand."

Nick's eyes flash with disappointment. "What don't you understand? First you don't want to see me anymore, then you lie to me about your cousins, and now you're surprised it's over?"

I can't believe this is really happening. I reach a hand out towards him, but he backs away like I've got cooties.

"Please, Nick." I'm begging now, but I don't care. "I had to lie. I was trying to protect you. You can't break up with me over a curse. Or maybe it's my hair? You don't like it short? Or maybe —"

He holds up his hands to stop me, sending droplets of water spraying onto my toes. "Stop, Dani. I really think it's all for the best. We probably should never have been together in the first place."

How can he say that? My cheeks start to burn, like his angry words have reached out and slapped them. This isn't how I planned for this conversation to go at all. I haven't even gotten a chance to tell him how I've been fighting off the Evil Eye. And all the things I've done to protect him. I clamp a hand defensively around my guitar string bracelet. Is he going to ask for it back now? My heart feels like someone's pushing it through a paper shredder.

"Are you serious?" My voice has shrunk to a pathetic whisper. "How can you say that?"

His eyes drop down to the surface of the water. "Come on, you know it wasn't the nicest thing to do to Kat. Especially with you two being friends and all. Didn't she get mad at you for going out with me?"

"Mad at me?"

He shrugs. "I thought girls got all jealous about stuff like that."

That's the point when my head begins spinning like one of those dizzy rides at the amusement park. You know, those ones that make you want to throw up? "What are you talking about? Why would Kat be jealous of me?"

Nick's eyebrows shoot up in surprise. "You mean she didn't tell you?"

"Tell me *what*?" I say, bracing my hands against the cedar deck. I have an eerie feeling that I'm not going to like his answer one bit.

Turns out I'm right.

"Our families have this, I guess you could call it an arrangement," he says, wiping a stray trickle of water from the end of his perfect nose. "They, well … they kind of promised Kat and me to each other when we were babies."

This time, I do fall over. "What?" I gasp as my butt hits the ground.

For a second, his face softens and he looks like the old Nick again — the one who adored me so much in Greece. He puts a hand out to help me up. But then pulls it back as he remembers the wall of anger that's still standing between us.

"I thought you knew," he says, his expression hardening again. "Why do you think it took me so long to ask you out? I knew it was wrong, but I liked you so much and so I went and did it. My mother was furious with me when I told her that I was going out with you. That's why I couldn't ask you over untilI knew they'd be out. I figured if I gave them some time, they'd get used to the idea of you and me. I really thought you were something special. And then I find out that you were cheating on me?"

Cheating? This is a total nightmare. I reach down and pinch my leg, praying the pain will wake me up and send me zooming back to reality. But of course it doesn't. "What are you talking about?" I squeak. "I never cheated. Who told you that?"

"I know you were flirting with other guys in Greece. And sneaking around with your old boyfriend here in Toronto. And that lame excuse about your family being in town?" His beautiful lips collapse into a pout. "If you'd just told me the truth, maybe we could have had a chance. And things wouldn't be so ugly now."

Are we ugly? Or is it just me? My hands fly up to cover my burning face. I want to hide, to run away and shut this whole dirty mess out. "I can't believe this is happening," I moan under my breath.

Nick's eyes darken. "So you admit it, then?" he says.

"No! Absolutely not! It's a lie!"

Call me crazy, but I swear I see a flicker of hope flash across his face. "Really?"

"Of course it is. Who's been telling you these things?"

He scoops a stray leaf out of the pool and lays it carefully out on the cedar deck to dry. "She asked me not to say anything."

Now *I'm* getting angry. "Come on, Nick! You owe me this much. Who told —" But my words trail off as the sordid pieces all start coming together. When he looks up again, I can see the answer to my question shining in his beautiful green eyes. And the truth makes me so sick to my stomach, I think I might hurl.

It all makes so much sense now. How can I have been so clueless? I stand up slowly and take a step back. My limbs feel limp and wobbly — like octopus legs. And my voice is barely more than a breath on my lips. "You don't have to answer, Nick. I know who it was."

Spinning around on my heels, I storm back through the house and leap onto my bike. I feel nauseous. I can't believe this. *She* gave me the Evil Eye. *She* poisoned my fish, stole my passport, destroyed my car, pushed those awful "cures" on me. She pretended she wasn't superstitious so I wouldn't suspect her. And it worked! How could I have been such a fool? I even let her chop off my hair and turn me ugly! And all because she's jealous. My whole body is shaking with anger.

How could she do this to me?

Chapter 18
• • • • • • •

"I need to speak to you in private. Now." My voice is shaking. I've never been this furious in my life.

Kat's brown eyes widen with surprise as she ushers me inside. "Sure. What is it?"

How can she stand there so innocently after everything she's done? I bite the inside of my cheek and force myself to wait until we're in her room. But the second the door closes, I let loose. "I can't believe it was you!"

Her mouth falls open. "Me?" she squeaks, clutching a hand to her chest. "W-what did I do?"

I stomp my foot on the floor. I wave my arms in the air. I'm so angry, I don't know what to do with myself. "You were jealous of me all along," I holler. "You poisoned my food in Greece, and it must have been you who loosened the strap on my sandal so I'd slip down that hill. And you stole my passport and egged my house and made my life hell through the awful 'cures.' You lied to me about that curse book I saw on your desk — it was yours all along, wasn't it? You were looking up ways to torture me. No wonder you were disappointed when I didn't agree to poke that girl's eyes out. It would have made you pretty happy to see me in jail, wouldn't it? And to do all this over a guy? I can't believe it! How could I have been so blind? This whole time, I thought you were my best friend!"

Kat's looking like she's been run over by a truck. I never knew she was *this* good of an actress. "What are you talking about?" she says. "I didn't ... I wouldn't ..."

"Stop!" I'm screaming now, but I can't help myself. "I can't believe you'd try to ruin my life like this! Why couldn't you have been honest with me from the start? Well, you can have Nick! I don't want him anymore. Have a nice life together. I'm calling the police right now and telling them who destroyed my car."

I take out my phone and start to dial: 9-1-—

She grabs my arm. "No, please don't. Okay, I admit I lied. I *am* totally superstitious. But you're always telling me how smart I am, and I know you think the superstitions are dumb, so I was just too embarrassed to tell you the truth. But I promise, the book you saw in my room was to *stop* the Evil Eye. You have to believe me, all I ever wanted to do was help!"

Something in her voice stops me from finishing the call. *She sounds sincere*, I think, my thumb hovering over the last button. I want to believe her so badly. But really, how can I? All the evidence is pointing to her. If it wasn't Kat who's been doing all these terrible things to me, then who? *No … no … it has to be her.*

"Why should I believe you when it all makes such perfect sense?" I ask, lowering my voice a notch. "Every time I talk about Nick, you act all weird and jealous. Like that day on the beach after our first date? Remember? That's when all my bad luck started. It wasn't the little girl we saw on our walk, was it? And it wasn't Costa either. There was never any Evil Eye. It was just you." Angry tears pool in my eyes, but I blink them away before she can see them. "I really thought you were my friend."

Kat squeezes her eyes shut. "I swear it wasn't me," she says. "I never liked Nick that way. We grew up like a brother and sister. It was my mother's big dream that we would get married. But I never … I mean … how could you think …" Her body starts to tremble so hard, for a second I think she's having a heart attack or something. "You just don't get it, do you?" she asks, her eyes still closed. "I can't believe I'm actually saying this," she whispers hoarsely.

"Saying what?" My thumb is still poised over the dial pad.

She takes a shuddery breath. Her body is still shaking like a scared kitten. "I don't want Nick. I never wanted Nick. I … I wanted … I wanted *you*!" Her eyes fly open and meet mine. Her face is like Jell-O. "There, I said it. Are you happy?" Her words fill the room like a storm cloud. It's probably the first time in my life that I've ever found myself utterly speechless.

Oh.

My.

God!

I struggle to unlock my throat. "You mean you're ... I mean ... you ... but ... Kat, I don't know what —" Before I know what's happening, she rises up on her tiptoes and lunges forward into my arms. Her tiny hands reach behind my neck and pull my mouth down to hers. I'm so stunned, I don't know what to say, or do, or think. I'm so shocked, I don't even remember to breathe. I just stand there and let her kiss me.

To be honest, it actually doesn't feel as strange as you might think. In some ways, it isn't all that different from kissing a boy. But in other ways, it's like I've been blasted onto an alien planet. The whole thing is just too awkward for me to handle. I mean, Kat's my friend. *What the heck is she doing?* After a couple of seconds, I regain my senses and push her off me gently. With my hand over my mouth, I stumble across the floor and sink down onto her bed, trying to process all this new information. I can feel the veins above my eyelids begin to pulse frantically. If there's ever a chance a person's head might actually explode from extreme pressure, this has to be it. A moment passes, and then I hear the sound of Kat's bare feet rushing to my side.

"Oh God, I'm sorry. Do you hate me?"

I can't answer her right away. My thoughts are swirling through my brain at warp speed. "No, of course I don't hate you," I finally whisper.

"Please don't be mad! You spent so much time talking about my first kiss — it was all I've been able to think about these past few weeks. I ... I just had to do it."

Holy moly, I'm her first kiss. She was never jealous. She never even liked Nick. She likes me!

"Get Lucky" goes off in my hands, interrupting my thoughts. I fumble for the talk button, grateful for an excuse to break away from Kat for a few seconds. I need a chance to get my thoughts sorted out. "Hello?" I gasp. After all that screaming, my voice is like sandpaper. I can barely manage to get the words out.

"Dani? Why do you sound so strange?"

"Hi, Mom. Sorry, Kat and I are just, um ... out for a jog," I croak.

"Sorry to interrupt, but I just got a phone call from the police department and I thought you'd want to hear what they said about Rosie."

I take a deep breath, trying to reclaim a bit of calm as I turn away from Kat. *Why is it that all life's crucial moments inevitably seem to happen at the same time?* "Okay, but quick, please."

"Remember the evidence collection they did on Rosie? They received the report back today. Turns out the weapon the attacker used was probably some kind of kitchen utensil — it was barely detectable, but the results are showing a slight coating of flour and butter at each of the entry points in the tire slashes and also on the gouges in the roof. There were no fingerprints but —"

My phone falls, exploding on impact into tiny pieces on the hardwood floor. I spin around to face Kat. My mouth opens but no sound comes out.

"Who was it?" she asks. "Dani? What's wrong?"

My skin feels like it's coated in a layer of ice. And my throat is so dry, I can't swallow. Is this what it feels like to be in shock? Shutting my eyes, I force out the awful truth.

Chapter 19

• • • • • • •

"There has to be some kind of explanation," Kat says between sobs. She's taking the news pretty hard. At first, she didn't want to believe me. But when I tell her about the police tests, she can't deny it anymore. That's when she starts to cry. "Maybe Mummy had a g-good r-reason?"

"A good reason? For attacking my car? Egging my house? Poisoning my food? Stealing my passport? Tell me, Kat, because I'm trying really hard to understand what could possibly justify all that." My words are raw again with anger. It's taking all my self-control to keep myself from screaming again.

"What do we do now?" Kat asks, between sobs. Her face is in her hands now.

"We confront her."

"And then what?" She peeks at me from between her fingers. Her big brown eyes are swimming with tears. She looks almost as upset as I feel. *It can't be easy finding out your own mother is a psychopath*, I think. Feeling my anger beginning to dissolve, I take her hand and pull her towards the door.

"We'll figure that out later. Come on, I'll do the talking."

"Wait!" she cries, pulling me back. "You're not going to tell Mummy about the kiss, are you?"

"Kat, I —"

"Please don't say anything to her. I've never told anybody my feelings. Especially not Mummy. She'll have a fit. She wants me to do the 'old country' thing and marry a Greek man and have a traditional Greek home. I don't know if I'm ready to take that away from her just yet."

I shake my head. "Don't worry, I won't say a word. Promise." Still holding hands, we go downstairs to the kitchen to confront Mrs. Papadakis. We find her standing by the sink cleaning a set of wooden-handled knives. Was it one of those that she used on Rosie? I'm furious just thinking about it. She smiles when she sees us.

"Hello, girls."

Dropping Kat's hand, I take a small step forward and gulp down the wad of nerves sticking in my throat. My pulse is hammering in my ears. "It's over. I know it was you," I say.

Mrs. P freezes. The room is dead silent except for the sound of running tap water. Placing the knives carefully into the drying rack, she turns off the faucet, wipes her dripping hands on her apron, and pivots around to face me. Her "sucking lemons" mouth is back. And her eyes are a pair of black holes.

"And how did you finally figure it out?" she asks. Her voice is eerily calm.

I step back until I'm standing beside Kat again. With a quivering hand, I point towards the large canister marked "flour" on the counter beside her. "You left your calling card all over my car."

Mrs. P shrugs. "You're smarter than you look."

My mouth drops open. *That's it? She's not even going to try and deny it?* I hear a loud gasp, but whether it came from Kat or me, I can't be sure. "So, it's true then? You admit it?" I ask.

She shrugs again as a smirk pulls at her lips. She looks about as guilty as a kid caught snooping for birthday presents.

"And do you also admit that you lied to Nick? That you tried to turn him against me by telling him I was flirting with other boys?"

The smirk vanishes and a shadow passes over Mrs. P's face. "Can you blame me?" she asks. The calm is gone. Now her voice is bristling with anger. "Nobody ever sees my daughter when she's with you. It's like she's invisible. Even in Greece — *our own* country — you were the centre of attention. You stole it all for yourself with your beautiful face and your fancy clothes. I tried very hard not to let it bother me. But when you tried to steal Nicholas away from my Katerina? That was just too much. For years I've known that this was the boy for my daughter."

I glance briefly over to Kat, who's frozen beside me. She's like one of those statues from the courtyard at the Olympic Palace. "Hang on," I say. "Did you ever ask either of them if they wanted to marry each other?"

Come on, this is your chance to tell her, Kat! I'm practically yelling at her with my eyes. But her gaze is so fixed on her mother that she doesn't even see me. I turn my attention back to Mrs. P. My question must have struck a nerve, because the veins in her temples are bulging and the skin on her neck is turning red.

"Hush up!" she hisses. "You know *nothing* about our life or our history! Our two families have been close for generations. We moved to Canada together, planned our futures together, helped and supported each other as we settled into this new country. Our children are *meant* to be together. But, of course, you don't understand any of this — how deeply the Greek ties run in our blood."

I shake my head and sigh. This whole mess is beginning to strike me as sad. So desperately sad. And in that instant, something changes inside of me and I'm not afraid of her anymore. Not a bit.

"We're not in Greece, Mrs. P," I say. "This is *Canada*. And we have laws in this country about destroying other people's property."

She clutches her apron, her knuckles popping white. "Don't talk to me about laws. Since the beginning of time, every girl in my family has married a Greek man. Nicholas has been promised to Katerina since they were babies. And you think you can sweep in and try to interfere with that? How dare you?"

That's when Kat finally speaks up. Her voice is quiet, but her eyes are glistening with rage. "Stop, Mummy. Just stop. I can't believe this is happening. How could you do this to Dani? The whole thing is sick!"

Mrs. P turns her attention over to her daughter. And for the first time, I can see a crack in that Greek warrior mask of hers.

"Katerina, I did this for you. How can a mother stand back and let someone else steal her daughter's future? When you get married and have a child of your own, you'll understand why I had—"

Kat's hands fly up to cover her ears. "Stop it! No! I'll never understand what you did to Dani. And here's a news flash — maybe I won't get married. Or have children either. Or maybe I will. But either way, it's going to be *my* choice. Not yours."

Mrs. P's mouth hangs open. From the gaping look of shock on her face, I guess that this must be the first time her daughter's ever defied her. Kat looks bigger and stronger than I've ever seen her look before. And she isn't trembling anymore. Maybe there's some Greek warrior in her blood too. *Go, Kat, go!* I cheer in my head.

"Did you ever think that I might want to do something else with my life?" she continues, clasping her thin hands to her heart. "Did you ever think of finding out what *I* wanted? I mean, you could have at least *asked* me if I wanted to marry Nick. That would have spared all of us a lot of trouble. Because if you had, I would have told you absolutely and positively *NO*."

"Katerina, please. You don't mean that."

"Stop! Would you just stop telling me what to think and start listening for a change? Nick is like my brother! How could anybody want to marry their brother? And how could you try to ruin someone's life just to ensure that I would marry someone Greek? Why is that such a big deal anyway? It's not like I'm going to forget where I came from."

You'd need a forklift to pick my jaw back up. I actually forget all about my own troubles while I watch her stand up to her mother. I was right when I said there's something magic about that first kiss. Look what's happening to Kat. It's like she's growing up right here and now. Right in front of us all.

"You weren't just hurting my friend, you know?" she continues. "You were hurting me too. Deceiving me all this time by giving me all those crazy cures to pass along to Dani. I can't believe you used me like that."

I wasn't planning on stepping back into the conversation, but I just can't help myself. "Yeah, that's right," I pipe up. "It was all a big lie. There was never any of that ridiculous Evil Eye."

"Be quiet," Mrs. P hisses, pointing a finger at me. A second later, she stomps to the sink, leans over, and spits like an angry cobra. *Ptoo-ptoo-ptoo*! When she's done, she stands up and turns back to look at me. "*Matiasma* is very real. Don't underestimate the role it might have played in your misfortunes."

This is the moment when everything becomes clear. Like someone's just opened a window inside my brain. I realize I have a choice to make. I can walk away from this awful woman. Or I can hold on to my anger and keep fuelling the fire of her jealousy.

No contest. I raise my hands in surrender. "Know what? I forgive you, Mrs. P."

The anger drains from her face. And just like that, I'm free. Evil Eye or just plain old-fashioned jealousy — whatever power she was holding over my life dissolves on the breath of those words. I straighten my shoulders and look over at Kat. Her face is the colour of ashes.

"What?" she cries. "You're letting her off the hook? After everything she's done?"

I nod. "Your mom's jealousy isn't my problem anymore."

"But what about Rosie? And all those awful things she did to you?"

"You're my best friend, Kat. I don't want you to have a mother in prison," I reply. "Just as long as she stays away from me and my family. Forever."

Kat spins around and faces her mother, her eyes dark with fury. "Well, *I'm* not letting you off the hook. You lied, you stole, and you hurt my friend. And all because you say you love me. If you really love me, you'll apologize to Dani."

"*Cardia mou*, you don't understand." She holds out her hands, palms up — like a convict begging for mercy. "I was just thinking of you and your future."

But the new, strong Kat isn't having it. "Apologize now, Mummy. Or so help me, I'll never speak to you again. And neither will Daddy, because I'll tell him everything you've done."

Mrs. P's face crumples. She slowly turns to me. Her eyes are so heavy, she can't lift them higher than my knees. "I am sorry for everything, Dani."

It's the first time she's said my name right. Her once steely voice is now a broken whine. She looks so pathetic in that moment, it almost makes me feel sorry for her. Almost.

Kat takes my arm and pulls me towards the door. "Let's get out of here. I'm going to help you explain this whole mess to Nick."

I let her lead me out of the kitchen. I walk out of that house feeling better than I've felt in weeks. Like I'm seeing the sun again after a long, dark thunderstorm. And the sky's filled with rainbows.

Epilogue

· · · · · ·

Nick was devastated after Kat and I explained everything. His golden-green eyes flashed with anger as he struggled to control his shock. "I'm so sorry, I had no idea. She's been like a second mother to me all these years. I — I never imagined she was capable of being so cruel." He took my hand and pulled me close. His palm cupped my cheek.

"Can you forgive me, Dani?"

Well, come *on*. Of course I forgave him. Wouldn't you? And would you really be surprised to find out that we've been together ever since?

Now I know what you're wondering — what about the kiss between me and Kat? Well, to tell you the truth, we haven't talked about it. Not even once. Although, just between you and me, I was flattered by the attention. Strangely enough, the kiss didn't hurt our friendship. In a weird way, it might have brought us closer. For the most part, that sad look seems to be gone from her eyes, which makes me happier than I can explain. And just last week, she told me that she took those romance novels out from the back of her closet and arranged them in a neat stack on her bookshelf. Right in plain sight. I don't think it'll be long before her other secret comes out too. Believe me, I'm not looking forward to seeing Mrs. P again. But when Kat's ready to tell her mother, I promised to be right there to support her.

Because that's what good friends do.

But you already knew that, right?

Yeah.

Acknowledgements
. . . .

Many thanks to the superhuman team at Dancing Cat Books —
Barry Jowett, Meryl Howsam, Bryan Ibeas, Andrea Waters,
Tannice Goddard, and Angel Guerra — for the tireless hours they
spend transforming rough manuscripts into beautiful books. A
special thank you to Cormorant Publisher Marc Côté for his
ongoing support and encouragement.

Thanks also to Gordon Pape, Kim Pape-Green, Sharon Jones,
Helene Boudreau, Helaine Becker and Tova Rich for agreeing to
read this story back when it was just a raw first draft (and for
generously telling me they liked it even then).

Heartfelt thanks to my loving home team, Jordy, Jonah, and
Dahlia — who cheer me on daily and come up with the magic
answers whenever I'm stuck.

Huge thanks to the Ontario Arts Council for supporting books
like this through the Writers' Reserve Program.

And finally, *efharisto para poli* to the Stavrinos sisters —

especially Joanne — for enthusiastically schooling me in all things Greek for the past thirty-five years.

Filakia.

About the Author
• • • • • • • • • • • •

Deborah Kerbel's latest young adult novel, Under the Moon (2012) was a finalist for the Governor General's Literary Award in the Children's Text category. Her other teen novels include Mackenzie, Lost and Found; Girl on the Other Side (nominated for the Canadian Library Association Young Adult Book Award, and Lure (nominated for the Manitoba Young Readers' Choice Award). A native of London, UK, Deborah now lives and writes in Thornhill, Ontario.